The En

Smorkus Flinders sm[illegible], showing a mouthful of craggy green teeth. With genuine pride, he said, "We're going to destroy the universe."

"They're mad," snorted Grakker. "Both of them. Or one is mad and the other is a fool."

Tar Gibbons frowned. "Perhaps not." Leaning forward, it asked, "Do you actually have a way to commit this horrible crime?"

Smorkus Flinders's smile grew even broader. "We're building a time bomb. All we need to finish it is Rod Allbright's—"

Before he could finish the sentence he gasped and began to make a strangled noise. His eyes rolled back in his head. He shuddered violently, then toppled with a crash, landing flat on his back.

"Rod Allbright's *what?*" I cried. "What do I have that you need?"

Books by Bruce Coville

The A.I. Gang Trilogy:
Operation Sherlock
Robot Trouble
Forever Begins Tomorrow

Bruce Coville's Alien Adventures:
Aliens Ate My Homework
I Left My Sneakers in Dimension X
The Search for Snout

Camp Haunted Hills:
How I Survived My Summer Vacation
Some of My Best Friends Are Monsters
The Dinosaur that Followed Me Home

Magic Shop Books:
Jennifer Murdley's Toad
Jeremy Thatcher, Dragon Hatcher
The Monster's Ring

My Teacher Books:
My Teacher Is an Alien
My Teacher Fried My Brains
My Teacher Glows in the Dark
My Teacher Flunked the Planet

Space Brat Books:
Space Brat
Space Brat 2: Blork's Evil Twin
Space Brat 3: The Wrath of Squat
Space Brat 4: Planet of the Dips

The Dragonslayers
Goblins in the Castle
Monster of the Year

Available from MINSTREL Books

BRUCE COVILLE'S ALIEN ADVENTURES

THE SEARCH FOR SNOUT

Illustrated by Katherine Coville

Published by POCKET BOOKS
New York London Toronto Sydney Tokyo Singapore

A MINSTREL PAPERBACK *Original*

A Minstrel Book published by
POCKET BOOKS, a division of Simon & Schuster Inc.
1230 Avenue of the Americas, New York, NY 10020

ISBN: 0-671-79834-0

First Minstrel Books paperback printing November 1995

10 9 8 7 6 5 4 3

Cover art by Stephen Peringer

Printed in the U.S.A.

For Kathy,
always and ever

CONTENTS

1. Home Is Where the Hurt Is 1
2. Family Conference 8
3. Missing: One Spaceship 19
4. Off to the Stars 27
5. Message from a Maniac 39
6. Chibling Rivalry 49
7. Crime and Punishment 59
8. A Voice from Beyond 69
9. Renegades of the Galaxy 79
10. Up from the Worm Farm 87
11. A Worm that Turned 99
12. Split Personality 109
13. Seymour 120
14. Into the Mentat 128
15. The Head Council 138

16. Roots 145
17. The Hall of Statues 152
18. Darker and Darker 163
19. The Belly of the Beast 173
20. The First Starfarers 182
21. Battle in the Beast 193
22. Seymour and I 202
Epilogue: Light-years to Go Before I Sleep 210

CHAPTER 1

Home Is Where the Hurt Is

YOU KNOW HOW SCARY IT IS TO GO HOME WHEN you're sure you're going to be in trouble?

Well, that's the way I felt the night the good ship *Ferkel* brought me back from Dimension X. I don't think I've ever been more frightened to go through my own front door.

In fact, I didn't go through it for a while. I just stood beside the hickory tree in our front yard, resting one hand on its rough bark and staring at the house.

The lights were still on in the upstairs room where the twins slept. I decided to put off going in until they were in bed. Dealing with Mom was going to be difficult enough. It would be easier to wait until morning to say what I had to say to Little Thing One and Little Thing Two.

The lights went out upstairs. Still I hesitated. Taking a deep breath of the sweet summer air, I listened to the crickets, watched the fireflies—all the while telling myself I would go in soon.

Soon, but not right this minute.

"Come on, Rod!" hissed my cousin Elspeth, who was standing a few feet behind me. "Let's move. The mosquitoes are killing me."

I sighed. Standing out here fussing wasn't going to change things. Or make them any easier. And if I didn't move soon, Elspeth would probably go in by herself—which would only make things even more complicated than they already were.

Taking a deep breath, I walked to the front door.

I put my hand on the knob, then hesitated.

Should I knock?

You don't usually knock to go into your own house, of course. But I had been away so long—and in such strange places—that it didn't quite feel like home here anymore.

As a matter of fact, considering what I was planning to do next, it *wasn't* really home anymore.

"Come on, Rod," urged Elspeth. "Open the door!"

"I don't want to frighten Mom. She's not expecting us. If I just open the door and walk in, it might scare her."

Before Elspeth could push past me and open the door herself, I reached forward and knocked.

No answer.

I knocked again, harder.

After a moment we heard footsteps. They stopped at the door and a familiar voice—a voice I had sometimes feared I would never hear again—called, "Who is it?"

I had a hard time answering because a lump had formed in my throat, and I had to push to get the words past it.

"Hello?" called my mother again, sounding nervous this time.

"It's me, Mom. Rod."

With a cry she flung open the door. "Rod! Where have you been? Are you all right?"

She threw her arms around me as if she was afraid I was going to vanish into the night. After she had held me tight for a minute, she drew back and whispered, "Is your father with you?"

I shook my head, wondering if she had any idea of the real truth about Dad.

She sighed. Looking past me, as if checking to see if maybe Dad was there after all, she noticed Elspeth. Disappointment and relief seemed to war for control of her face. All she said was, "Thank goodness you're here, too, sweetheart! Your parents have been so worried!"

A few weeks earlier I would have been tempted to say, "Worried? I would think they would be relieved!" After all, if they gave a Nobel prize for "Achievement in Being a Pain in the Neck," Elspeth would probably be the world's top contender. But the two of us had been through so much together in Dimension X that I had sort of gotten used to her.

Before I could say anything at all, we were interrupted by an explosion of gray fur, accompanied by yips of delight and a frenzy of tail wagging and face licking.

"Bonehead!" I cried. "How ya doin', boy?"

Without waiting for Bonehead to finish greeting me, my mother hustled us inside. She closed the door firmly behind her, as if to make sure that we couldn't get back out again. Then she leaned against the doorway. Her shoulders began to shake as she watched Bonehead bounce around my legs. When I looked closer, I realized she was crying.

Let me tell you—when it comes to sheer guilt, nothing beats making your mom cry.

And we hadn't even gotten to the hard stuff yet. How was she going to react when she saw what I had in my pocket?

Before I could worry about that, she whispered, "Rod, where have you been? Did you really go off with your father? *Where is he?*"

I started to answer, but we were interrupted again, this time by the twins. Little Thing One (sometimes called Linda, but mostly by my mother) burst through the door shouting, "Roddie! Roddie! Roddie!"

Pigtails streaming behind her, she came barreling toward me.

Little Thing Two (Eric for short) was hard on her heels. "Roddie, you came back!" he called.

Each of them grabbed one of my legs. Clinging to my knee as if she was afraid I was going to vanish on the spot, Linda cried, "Where did you go? You're a naughty Roddie. You made Mommy cry."

"Naughty, naughty Roddie!" agreed Eric. "You weren't here to bop us with our teddy bears at bedtime. I couldn't go to sleep at night!"

This was getting worse by the minute.

I looked around at our cozy old kitchen—the worn blue linoleum; our faithful cookie bear, where Mom stored her home-baked treats; the noisy refrigerator, still covered by my school papers that Mom had stuck to it with fruit-shaped magnets. Suddenly I felt as if someone had grabbed my heart and was starting to squeeze. How could I possibly leave again, now that I had made it back here?

But how could I not, given the startling information I had learned in Dimension X?

Dropping to my knees I hugged the twins, trying not to cry myself.

"Where did you go?" asked Little Thing One

again. She sounded sympathetic, now that she could see how upset I was.

"We had a terrifying adventure," said Elspeth.

"I want one!" said Little Thing Two.

"Was it with Grakker?" asked Little Thing One.

My mother sighed. "These two have been talking about those imaginary aliens ever since you went off with your father, Rod. Please tell them the truth."

I glanced at Elspeth. She made a face that seemed to say, "Don't look at me. She's *your* mother."

I took a deep breath. Mom was going to have to know the truth sooner or later.

It might as well be now.

So I reached into my shirt pocket . . . and took out the aliens.

CHAPTER 2

Family Conference

"GRAKKER!" CRIED LITTLE THING ONE, CLAPPING her hands.

"And Madame Pong!" added Little Thing Two.

My mother sighed. "They're just toys," she told the twins sharply.

"Uh-uh," said Little Thing One. "They're real. Ask Roddie."

My mother turned to me, an exasperated look on her face. "Rod, will you please tell them the truth?"

Setting Grakker and Madame Pong gently onto the counter, I said, "Wel-l-l-l-l . . . the truth is, the twins are right."

Mom started to say something, and I could tell from her face that it was going to be kind of cranky. I actually felt bad when she stopped herself from snapping at me, because I knew she was holding back out of fear that if she said something wrong, I might disappear again. After a moment she said, very calmly, "Rod, please. I don't want you getting the twins all wound up in some . . . some . . ."

Looking past me to the shelf where the aliens stood, she gasped, then put her hand to her mouth and staggered backward.

Madame Pong had put her long, yellow hands together and was making a graceful bow. "Please do not be alarmed, Mrs. Allbright," she said softly. "We bring you greetings from the stars."

Grakker snorted. Given how cranky he could be, I was glad that was all he did. I just hoped he would remember his promise not to use his ray gun in the house.

Mom's head swiveled back and forth between me and the tiny aliens so fast it looked as if she were watching a Ping-Pong game.

"Rod?" she whispered hoarsely. "How did you do that?"

"They're real, Mom," I said gently. "Friends of mine."

I didn't add the biggest news, which was that while I hadn't actually gone off with Dad (as Madame Pong had said in the letter she left behind to cover my absence), the aliens claimed to know something about what had happened to him.

One thing at a time would do for now.

"We have to talk, Mrs. Allbright," said Madame Pong.

Mom nodded, unable to answer. The twins scurried to the counter and put their hands on the edge of it, struggling to get their faces high enough to see the aliens.

"Greetings, Larvae," said Grakker.

Madame Pong shot him a sharp glance, then turned back to the twins and said, "How pleasant to see you again, young ones."

She was dressed, as usual, in an open, high-collared robe whose color moved through a range of purples and blues, depending on how the light hit it. Beneath the robe she wore a long lavender shift. Her large, pointed ears framed a high-domed, bald head. She was slender and graceful.

Grakker, on the other hand, looked like a refugee from the World Wrestling Federation. His bulky, muscular body was covered by a uniform that was mostly red, with yellow-gold highlights. His green face looked something like a gorilla's might if you shaved off all its hair and stuck a pair of tiny horns on its forehead. Even though he was just about the crankiest being I had ever met, I had grown to respect him—even kind of like him—during our various adventures.

Little Thing One started to reach for him, then thought better of it. I could tell she was remembering the last time she had tried to pick him up.

Little Thing Two leaned close to the aliens and whispered, "Thank you for bringing Roddie back."

Madame Pong smiled and nodded. Considering our plans, I was surprised she could do that without getting a guilty look on her face. I sure would have. But then, I could barely lie to save my own life. She was a professional diplomat, and it was part of her job to hide her feelings when necessary.

Looking up at my mother, Madame Pong said, "Perhaps we could go into your living room and sit down? I have to apologize for our size, by the way. I felt it would be better for us to come in with Rod, and we couldn't really do that at our full height without alarming you more than we already have."

She didn't mention that even at full height the aliens still only came up to about my waist. Grakker considered that some sort of top-secret information.

Mom moved briefly into hostess mode. "Can I get you anything?" she asked. "Some coffee, or tea, or . . ."

Her attempt at pretending things were normal didn't last long. Her voice trailed off, and she waved her hands in confusion.

"We're fine," said Madame Pong with a smile.

"Uh—do you want us to carry you?"

"We'd rather fly," said Grakker. Activating his rocket belt, he zoomed into the air, then said, "Lead the way, Deputy Allbright."

"Deputy?" asked my mother.

"Yeah, deputy," said Elspeth bitterly. "Rod has all the luck. I wish *my* father was a—"

She fell silent. For a moment I wondered if she had had a momentary attack of common sense. Then I realized that Madame Pong had also launched herself into the air. Unlike Grakker, she had flown straight toward Elspeth, which had startled her into closing her mouth long enough to remember that she wasn't supposed to say anything about my father.

That was to be Madame Pong's job.

"You wish your father was a *what,* Elspeth?" asked my mother sharply.

"A good guy," said Elspeth, quickly if unconvincingly.

Mom was clearly suspicious of this answer, but held off on her questions when Madame Pong said, "Please, let us go to the other room to talk. All—or at least as much as we know—will be explained in time."

My mother nodded, and we went into the living room.

Grakker and Madame Pong stationed themselves on the coffee table. Madame Pong stood.

Grakker sat on the spine of a mystery novel. The twins crouched eagerly at the end of the table. I could tell they were dying to get their hands on the little aliens, but that they knew better than to try.

Mom sat on the love seat, right in front of the coffee table. So she was pretty close to the aliens, too. Elspeth and I sat on either side of her. I could see Mom's hands shaking, which only made me feel more like slug slime than I did already. Putting them on her knees to stop the trembling, she said, "All right, tell me everything."

So we did, starting with the first time I met the aliens, which was when they crashed through my bedroom window and landed in the papier-mâché I was using for my school project. There were a lot of interruptions and questions along the way, of course—including one when Mom apologized to Grakker for the time she had picked him up because she thought he was a toy and she wanted me to give him back to Billy Becker.

Mom kept glancing at me through all this. When she found out that Billy Becker was really an incredibly vicious intergalactic villain named BKR*, she apologized to me as well, for trying to make me be nice to him all those times.

She got pretty upset when we told her how

*Pronounced "Bee Kay Are"—Rod.

Smorkus Flinders had kidnapped me and Elspeth into Dimension X in order to get revenge on Grakker.

Grakker himself got upset when we told Mom about how Flinge Iblik, our Master of the Mental Arts (also known as "Snout," because of his long purple face) had mysteriously faded away while we were in Dimension X.

But it was when we got to the end of the story that things really went over the edge. I was trying to explain why the aliens had been flying near our house to begin with. Looking carefully at Mom, I said, "So I take it you didn't know the truth about Dad?"

"What truth?" she asked sharply.

"Man," said Elspeth. "Uncle Art was even sneakier than *my* Dad."

"He wasn't sneaky!" I snapped. "He had his reasons."

"Rod," said my mother. "What are you talking about?"

Madame Pong stepped forward. "Mrs. Allbright, I am sure your husband had his reasons for not telling you, but the time has come for you to know the truth. Your husband was . . . well . . . not of this world."

My mother looked from the aliens to me, from me to the aliens.

Then she fell off the love seat.

I knew how she felt. I had been pretty boggled myself when I found out Dad was from outer space. Of course, in Mom's case, it only meant that she had *married* an alien. In my case, it means I *am* part alien—though even that turned out to be more complicated than I expected.

When we finally got Mom sitting up again, she asked me to make her a cup of tea. I was glad to, since it provided a good excuse for everyone to be quiet for a while. When I brought her the tea, she waited for it to cool, then took three long, slow sips before she was ready to talk again. Even then the cup rattled as she placed it back on the saucer. Finally she looked at Madame Pong.

"Are you seriously telling me that my husband is an alien?"

"Perhaps *alien* is an unfortunate word. I would prefer to say he is a citizen of the galaxy."

My mother snorted. "So am I."

Madame Pong looked a little uncomfortable, which was unusual for her. "Strictly speaking, that is not true. After all, Earth is not part of the League of Worlds."

My mother's nostrils flared, the way they do when she thinks someone is insulting her. "Let's not split hairs. The point is, Art wasn't human. Is that right?"

Madame Pong nodded.

Mom sighed. "The worst thing about this is that I can just hear my parents saying 'I told you so' when they find out. All right, tell me the rest. Why was he here? Am I some sort of experi—" She broke off. Her eyes wide, she looked from me to the twins, then back again.

"The kids!" she said hoarsely. *"What about the kids?"*

"Oh, they have full galactic citizenship," said Madame Pong.

"That's not what I meant! What does this mean for them? How weird are they going to be?"

"How weird was your husband?"

"Plenty!" Mom relaxed a little and actually smiled. "But then, that was part of why I loved him." She sat up straight again, and I could see that ideas and questions were zooming in and out of her brain faster than she could keep track of them. "But why did he marry *me?* And why did he leave?"

"Love is a great mystery," said Madame Pong. "Why he married you, I cannot say—though for him to marry a nongalactic citizen is a serious thing, and I suspcct indicates a very deep connection. Why did he leave? I cannot answer that, either, except to tell you that we have reason to believe it was not voluntary."

Mom's eyes grew still wider. "He was kidnapped?" she asked in horror.

"That is one possibility. Or it could be that he fled Earth in order to lure some menace away from you and the children. It may even be that he was drawn away by some unexpected but urgent duty."

My mother nodded. Duty was something she understood. She was always doing something or other—helping out at church, taking a meal to a sick neighbor, volunteering at school—because she thought it was her duty. It used to be that I wished she would stay home more. Now I was starting to have a different idea of duty myself.

"Why was he here to begin with?" asked Mom.

Madame Pong spread her arms. "I assume it had something to do with BKR. However, the opposite could also be true, that BKR was here because of your husband. Please remember, Mrs. Allbright, Captain Grakker and I are not the leaders of the galaxy, but merely its servants. On some matters, not all is made known to us. Much of this is a mystery to us as well as you."

She had pretty much told me the same thing. It was very frustrating, because there was so much I wanted to know about my father: not just why he was here, but who he really was, his whole life story. But all the crew could tell me was that Dad was "well thought of at the highest levels of the galaxy."

"That's all I know, Rod," Madame Pong said

apologetically after I had asked her about Dad for the seventh or eighth time. "You must understand that there are many levels of power above me. Information is not always easy to come by."

Of course, when I thought about it, I hadn't cared that much about Dad's life story back when I thought he was just an earthling. Like most of my friends, I knew a little bit about my parents' past, but I had never really asked them about it, never really tried to find out who they were. I always thought it was sad that both Dad's parents were gone—he had never said "dead" I realized, just "gone"—but I hadn't given it much more attention. He was my dad, and that was enough.

Until he disappeared.

I had been angry at him for so long for abandoning us that even now, when I knew the truth, I sometimes had to remind myself he hadn't just run off, that something far stranger was going on. It's weird how anger can stay with you, even when the reason for being angry is gone.

Anyway, the aliens were looking for my father, which was exactly what Madame Pong was saying to my mother: "We are about to embark on a search for your husband, Mrs. Allbright."

"Good," whispered Mom. "I miss him."

Madame Pong nodded and rolled right on to her next point, the big one:

"We want to take Rod with us."

CHAPTER 3

Missing: One Spaceship

I HAD SEEN MY MOTHER GET ANGRY BEFORE, BUT pretty much that meant her eyes got kind of scary and tight lines appeared beside her mouth. I had rarely heard her raise her voice. So though I expected her to object to this idea, I was pretty surprised when she slammed both fists on the coffee table and shouted at the top of her lungs, "No! Absolutely, positively not!"

Grakker and Madame Pong flew up from the table. I think it was the force of Mom's pounding that sent them into the air. But they both immediately switched on their rocket belts and shot up to the ceiling, where they hovered until Mom had settled down a little.

I was surprised that Grakker didn't pitch a fit of his own, and wondered which module Madame Pong had put in the back of his skull before we left the ship.

Mom was just getting warmed up. "You have got to be out of your minds!" she shrieked. "I am *not* sending my son off into outer space with a group of . . . *foreigners!*"

The twins had scooted back from the table and were hiding behind an armchair. Little Thing Two was crying—not loudly, just a few tears rolling down his cheeks.

"I told you she wouldn't like the idea," whispered Elspeth, as if this had been some brilliant prediction.

Before I could tell her to shut up, my mother turned to me and said, "Rod, did you know about this?"

At the moment all I knew was that I would rather be put through a meat grinder than have to deal with this kind of uproar.

"Rod . . . ?"

She wasn't going to let go of it.

She was also the one who had trained me to tell the absolute truth under all circumstances, no matter how dangerous it might be. For reasons of survival, this was something I was trying to get over. But I certainly hadn't progressed far enough to be able to lie to *her* when she asked a direct question. Probably never would.

So I swallowed hard and said, "I want to go find Dad."

I could almost hear the buzzer go *BLAT! Wrong Answer!*

"Go to your room, young man!" cried my mother.

I sighed. I had triumphed in hand-to-hand combat with the most horrible creature in Dimenson X, and I was being sent to my room?

What was even more ridiculous was that I stood up to go.

Well, I guess it wasn't that silly. It was a good reason to get out of the living room, which at the moment felt even scarier than Dimension X.

Didn't work, though. Madame Pong said what I had been unwilling to. Her voice gentle but firm, she said, "Mrs. Allbright, Rod has been through a great deal since you last saw him. He is now an honored member of the Galactic Patrol."

"He's my *baby!*" shouted Mom.

"That he is," agreed Madame Pong. "But there is a time when the child must leave the home and enter the wider world."

"Well, that time isn't now. He has to stay home and . . . and get an education!"

Madame Pong shook her head and smiled sadly. "What better education for a young person than to travel the galaxy? Think of it, Mrs. Allbright. We will show your son the weeping forests of Kryndamar, take him to hear the singing waters of Farallan. We will carry him with us to planets strange and wondrous, introduce him to life forms beyond your imagination. You live on a beautiful world, Mrs. Allbright. But it is, all in all, a very small part of the galaxy. Let Rod come with us, and we'll show him worlds beyond worlds beyond worlds, give him an education more far reaching than anything available here on Earth."

"I want to go, too!" shouted Little Thing One.

"Me too, me too!" cried Little Thing Two.

I tried to shush them before they got Mom even more upset than she was already.

Ignoring the twins, Madame Pong said, "Moreover, as we told you during our briefing, our Master of the Martial Arts, Tar Gibbons, has made Rod its *krevlik*. This is a rare honor, Mrs. Allbright, and it has already been much to Rod's benefit."

Mom looked at me. Adventures can be pretty rough on a person, but given the shape I had been in when I left, a little roughness hadn't been a bad idea. While I was gone I had lost a lot of my pudge and grown some extra muscles, which had to be clear to her.

What she hadn't noticed yet was how much better I could *move*. At school my nickname had been "Rod the Clod"—which was a little cruel, but very accurate.

I still had moments of clumsiness. But Tar

Gibbons had taught me a lot about how to move gracefully—not to mention how to protect myself from bullies.

Even though I *wanted* to go with the aliens, the idea of leaving my family was almost ripping my heart out. So I could imagine what it must be doing to Mom. But when it came right down to it, the question wasn't how hard it was on me, or Mom, or the twins.

The bottom line was, my father was in trouble, and I had every intention of going out there to find him.

Before I could say that we were interrupted by a splatter of light against the window.

Looking up, my mother once again cried out in astonishment.

The *Ferkel* was floating outside. The little spaceship bumped gently against the glass, as if asking to be let in.

The plan had been for the ship to stay out of sight until the meeting with my mother was finished, no matter how long it took. If Tar Gibbons and Phil had decided to change that, it must mean something serious was going on.

Without waiting for Mom to okay things, I went to open the window.

Much to the delight of Little Thing One and Little Thing Two, the ship floated into the room.

Grakker, who did not deal well with changes of plan, was not at all delighted. In fact, he was furious, something I could tell from the way his nostrils were opening and closing.

The ship settled onto the coffee table. A door opened in its side, and a ramp extended downward.

"Excuse me," said Grakker, flying down to the table. "I will return shortly."

He stomped up the ramp.

We all stared at the ship, wondering what was going on.

It couldn't have been more than two minutes before Grakker stomped back out, more upset than ever. "We have to leave," he snapped.

"Now?" cried Madame Pong in astonishment.

"Now."

"Why?"

Grakker paused. He looked around the room suspiciously, then said, "By Galactic Ordinance Number 135.379.744 I am swearing you all to silence. Disobedience is punishable in ways of which it is better not to speak. Do you understand?"

We all nodded, even the twins.

Turning back to Madame Pong, Grakker said, "The *Merkel* has vanished!"

"Merkel! Merkel! Merkel!" said Little Thing One.

"Perkel! Perkel! Perkel!" said Little Thing Two, who couldn't stand to be left out.

As for me, I felt a cold chill of dread. The *Merkel,* another ship of the patrol, had been carrying our old enemy, BKR. Did this mean the little beast was on the loose again?

That would have been horrible news all by itself, of course. But what made things worse—far worse, from my point of view—was that just a day earlier we had been told BKR knew something about what had happened to my father. Our plan had been to head for the *Merkel* as soon as we left my house so we could question BKR.

I realized now that I had built up that meeting in my mind to the point where I was convinced BKR would tell us exactly where to find my father. The news that the ship was missing made me feel as if I had been punched in the stomach.

"What happened?" I asked.

Grakker's scowl deepened. "The ship had made a routine stop on a planet called Zambreno. Shortly after it left, its radio broadcasts were cut off. It has not been heard from since. We are ordered to go search for it immediately."

Madame Pong looked grim. "I am sorry, Mrs. Allbright. But we must go, and we must go now. It is vital that Rod come with us."

My mother crossed her arms and shook her head. "Absolutely not!"

Madame Pong closed her eyes again. Then, her voice little more than a whisper—almost as if she was apologizing for what she had to say—she hit Mom with the one argument she couldn't possibly resist.

CHAPTER 4

Off to the Stars

"MRS. ALLBRIGHT, IT PAINS ME TO TELL YOU THIS, BUT I have reason to believe Rod may have a psychic link to his father."

Mom looked at her warily. "So?"

Madame Pong spread her arms, as if indicating this was all beyond her control. "Well, you must see what that means. Rod's presence on the *Ferkel* could spell the difference between success and failure in our long-term mission." She paused, then whispered for emphasis. "The difference between finding your husband or not."

My mother put her hand to her mouth, then collapsed, sagging against the couch like a balloon that had lost its air.

Given everything that had happened to hcr in the last couple of hours—my unexpected return, meeting a pair of miniature aliens, learning that the man she had married was *also* from outer space—I could see why Mom would accept this idea so easily. Oddly enough, I found *myself* wondering whether Madame Pong was actually telling the truth, or just spinning out a story in order to convince my mother to let me go.

I felt a little guilty keeping quiet about my suspicions. But I had to find my father, and one way or another I planned to be on the *Ferkel* when it left.

Besides, I had already received a message from Snout inside my head, so I knew that such a psychic link was possible. And I *was* part alien. So who could tell what weird abilities I might have? Maybe Madame Pong really was telling the truth.

After a long time my mother nodded. Her voice seeming to come from somewhere far away, she whispered, "If that's really the case, I guess Rod had better go with you."

Madame Pong smiled serenely. Then, seeing the stricken look on my mother's face, she lifted a finger and said, "A moment, please." Turning to Grakker, she pulled him aside and whispered into his ear.

His face got tight. "Absolutely not!" he roared.

Madame Pong continued talking. Finally Grakker growled, "All right, all right. But it must be brief. *Very* brief!"

Madame Pong turned to my mother. "On behalf of the crew I would like to invite you and your . . . things . . . to take a brief tour of the *Ferkel*, so you can see where Rod will be living."

My mother looked at the tiny ship.

"We'll shrink you," said Madame Pong. "If we had more time, I would prefer going outdoors and enlarging the ship. That way you might feel less nervous about this. Alas, we do not have the time to spare. But Captain Grakker has graciously agreed to let you aboard while we prepare for departure."

"Yes!" said my mother, suddenly, eagerly, as if her voice had been missing and just returned. "Of course."

All this happened so fast I nearly forgot one of the things I had meant to do when I came back. "Wait!" I cried. "I have to get something."

"Don't forget your toothbrush, Rod!" called my mother as I raced toward my room. "And pack some clean underw—"

"Mom!"

I heard Madame Pong begin to talk to Mom, and figured she was explaining how the ship would provide things like new clothes for me.

When I got to my room, I saw at once that Mom had cleaned it while I was gone. For some reason that really got to me. The place didn't look lived in anymore, and as I paused at the door, it suddenly hit me deep in the stomach that I might never see my home again. I actually staggered as a wave of fear and sorrow washed over me. My certainty that I had to go with the aliens began to dissolve.

Then Grakker came flying up, cranky and shouting for me to hurry, and I had no more time to hesitate. Scrambling through my stuff, I found the gifts the aliens had given me after our first adventure. One was a book called *Secrets of the Mental Masters,* which had come from Snout.

The second was a ring from Madame Pong.

Because of Mom's cleanup job, it took me longer to find them than it normally would have.

Once I had them, I hurried back to the living room.

The aliens had already shrunk my mother, the twins, and Elspeth. Mom and Elspeth were about two inches high, just like the aliens. The twins were only an inch high, which made them incredibly cute—especially since they were running around in circles shouting, "I'm tiny! I'm tiny!"

I stepped into position so that I could be shrunk, too. Then we all climbed the little ramp that led into the ship.

Tar Gibbons and Phil were in the control room when we entered. Even though we had told Mom about these two aliens, she seemed pretty startled when she actually saw them.

I could understand. The Tar is a strange-looking character. It's shaped like a lemon with legs—four legs, to be exact. It also has two arms, a long neck, and big goggly eyes. It is my teacher and I love it. But I'd be the first to admit that it's pretty weird to look at.

Mom handled it pretty well. "Pleased to meet you, Mr. Gibbons," she said, extending her hand.

Elspeth laughed. "It's not a mister, it's a *tar.*"

Seeing Mom's confusion, Madame Pong added, "Roughly translated, *Tar* means 'Wise and beloved warrior who can kill me with his little finger if he should so desire.' It is a title of great honor."

"How nice," said Mom uneasily.

"And this is Phillogenous esk Piemondum," I said quickly, pointing to the large potted plant floating next to the Tar.

"My, what a beautiful blossom you have," said Mom admiringly.

"Thank you," replied Phil, who spoke by "burping" through air pods that grew close to his stem. He extended one of his leaves, and Mom politely put her hand out to shake it.

The leaf came off in her hand.

"Oh, my god, I'm so sorry!" she cried. She started trying to hand it back to him.

"Do not worry, Mrs. Allbright," said Madame Pong, placing a gentle hand on my mother's

shoulder. "Phil was done with that leaf. Giving it to you is a sign of great honor."

My mother swallowed hard, then seemed to collect herself. Nodding graciously, she said, "Thank you very much, Mr. Piemondum."

We had barely finished the greetings when a ball of purple fur bolted into the room and wrapped itself around my leg. "Eeee-e-e-eep!" it wailed. "Eeeep! Eeeep! Eeeep!"

"A kitty-critter!" cried Little Thing One. She tried to pry it off my leg, but this only caused the ball of fur to cling more tightly. "I want it, Roddie!"

"No, *I* want it!" said Little Thing Two, latching on as well. "Let *me* have it!"

"I take it this is the chibling you told us about?" asked my mother, somehow managing to separate the kids from my leg as she spoke.

I nodded. I knew the little creature would let go of me in a few minutes. It had bonded with me in Dimension X, and it got upset whenever I had to leave it alone. Like Elspeth, it was kind of annoying, but not so bad once you got used to it.

The tour was a great success, at least as far as the twins were concerned. They must have said "Wow!" and "Coolie-dookers!" a hundred times. Of course, what impressed them were simple things like flashing lights and things that made noise.

What impressed my mother was Phil's explanation of how the *Ferkel* managed to cover interstellar distances by taking shortcuts through other dimensions.

Not everyone enjoyed the tour. Grakker muttered and grumbled the whole time, crossing and uncrossing his arms and generally acting cranky and impatient. He kept contacting Phil to see if the ship was ready to go, and mumbling about "interfering earthlings," as if we were somehow slowing down the preparations.

"I really must requisition a new patience module for him," Madame Pong whispered to me. "He's short-circuited his way through our entire inventory."

Elspeth was almost as bad. She complained so much about the fact that I got to go with the aliens while she was stuck on Earth that finally even my mother got fed up. "Oh, for heaven's sake, Elspeth," she snapped. "Stop whining!"

As for me, I got a big charge out of showing off the ship. The *Ferkel* was pretty cool. Each of the aliens had a room designed to suit his, her, or its specific needs, so there was a lot of variety. My favorite was Tar Gibbons's room, which contained a small, mist-shrouded pond.

Mom preferred Madame Pong's chamber,

which was filled with gauzy, multicolored hangings that made it look as if a rainbow cloud had settled inside.

Phil's room was something like a jungle; if he had been there, it would have been hard to tell him from the nonintelligent plants. (Or maybe they were *all* intelligent. Who could tell?)

What really turned on the twins was the recreation room, which had the most fabulous games you could imagine.

Since I was the junior member of the crew, my own cabin was fairly small. But I did have a computer hookup (and what a computer!), my own bathroom, and an antigravity bed. I really loved this idea. A lot of mattress companies promise that using their bed will be like sleeping on air. I really would be! Only I hadn't actually had a chance to try it out yet, because we had come straight home from Dimension X, and I had yet to spend my first night—or sleep period, since there was no real day and night in space—on the ship.

Mom approved of my room, and did seem to feel better for knowing where I was going to live. What made her feel even better was the discovery that the ship had a chapel. At least, that was the best word the aliens' language program could come up with for it. Madame Pong said its use was actually somewhat more complicated than that word would indicate.

Anyway, it was a small room, quiet and dimly lit, that was reserved for contemplating matters of the spirit.

"I do not know why you are surprised that we have such a place, Mrs. Allbright," said Madame Pong. "Such things are universal concerns."

The one thing I noticed that Madame Pong *didn't* show Mom and the twins—and I certainly didn't suggest it—was the room at the bottom of the ship where we were holding Smorkus Flinders in suspended animation. I was pretty sure if my mother actually saw the horrible monster I had been forced to battle, she would really wig out.

All too soon Phil announced that the ship was ready to go.

"Time is up!" snapped Grakker. He bowed stiffly to my mother and said, "I'm sorry Mrs. Allbright, but we have to leave *now!* Madame Pong, I will be in the conference room. As soon as we cross dimensions, gather the crew for a meeting."

He turned and stalked away.

My mother was silent, but the look on her face was like an arrow through my heart.

"Roddie!" cried the twins, attaching themselves to my legs like a pair of chiblings. "Don't go, Roddie!"

I felt as if I might as well just rip my heart out of my chest and cut it in two. If only I could be two people: one who stayed home with the family, and one who went off into the world to have adventures. But the fact was, there was only one of me. Whether I stayed with Mom and the twins or went off to look for Dad, half my heart would be hurting.

Things moved fast after that, with Phil sounding an alarm and announcing that all visitors had to leave the ship at once.

When Mom hugged me good-bye at the door I could feel her tears falling onto my face. Looking past me to Madame Pong, she said fiercely, "You take good care of him, do you hear? I want you to bring him home safe, and his father with him. I want my men back!"

Madame Pong bowed respectfully.

"I honor the mother spirit within you," said Tar Gibbons, blinking its enormous eyes. "Mothers must be as fierce as warriors."

My mother gave me another big hug and whispered, "I love you, Rod." Then she pulled back, looked me in the eyes, and said firmly, *"Make me proud of you."*

Taking the twins by the hands, she turned and

walked from the ship with great dignity and pride. As soon as they were off the ramp, we gave them a dose of the enlarging ray.

Then we shot up from the coffee table and sailed through the window.

Watching through the viewscreen, I saw my mother waving frantically for us to come back. The sight tore at my heart. But there was no turning back now. Less than a minute later I felt the little jolt that indicated the ship was shifting dimensions, and I knew we were truly on our way.

It wasn't until later that night that I realized exactly why Mom had been signaling for us to come back.

CHAPTER 5

Message from a Maniac

AS SOON AS WE REACHED A PLACE WHERE IT WAS SAFE to put the ship on autopilot, we gathered in the conference room, as the captain had ordered. We sat in a semicircle around a glossy black table.

Actually, I stood off to the side at first. When Madame Pong motioned for me to take a seat, I realized just how serious they were about having me be a member of the crew. Calling me "Deputy" Allbright was no joke. I had truly become a member of the Galactic Patrol.

His face even grimmer than usual, Grakker said, "I did not tell you the entire contents of our message from Galactic Headquarters because I did not want to upset Mrs. Allbright more than necessary. Besides, this is highly classified information. The truth is, we did not merely lose contact with the *Merkel.* It was highjacked by BKR, who stranded the crew on the Zambreno's third moon, then disappeared with their ship."

Grakker's scowl deepened. "Before he went, BKR gave them a message to deliver to us."

He looked down at a sheet of paper he held in his hand (well, it wasn't actually paper, but that's the easiest way to describe it), then read us the following:

"To the crew of the *Ferkel:*

"So sorry to learn you escaped from Dimension X alive. It's a nice place to die.

"On the other hand, you got back just in time for some exciting developments. I'm about to put the finishing touches on a new project that will be the most horrible thing I have ever created.

"Madame Pong, I know that when you talk about me, you are fond of saying 'millions have wept.' I fear you will have to revise your estimate upward, my dear. I sneer at the tininess of my past efforts. This time when I am done, millions *times* millions will weep.

"Or perhaps not. When I complete this project, it may well be that the entire galaxy is beyond weeping.

"This is so deliciously evil it gives me chills just thinking about it.

"If you want to stop me, you'll have to

catch me. I left a little clue for you on Zambreno—just to keep things interesting. No fun if you don't at least have a chance. A *last* chance, perhaps I should say.

"Grakker, if you're reading this out loud—see, I know how you operate, dear boy—I would appreciate it if you could insert an evil laugh for me at this point.

"That's all for now, kids. See you at the end of time.

"Or maybe not.

BKR

"P.S. to Rod Allbright: Give it up, Porky. Once a pudge-boy, always a pudge-boy."

Madame Pong made a gesture of contempt. "What a despicable *binderzunk!* He makes me want to do something rude."

I looked at her in astonishment and almost wished she would do something rude, just so I could see it.

Stretching its neck forward, Tar Gibbons said, "Captain, may I suggest that this might be an appropriate time to interrogate our prisoner?"

"Absolutely," agreed the captain. "You and your krevlik can go fetch him."

At a nod from the Tar, I followed it out of the room. We went to the bottom of the ship, to a room filled with egg-shaped green pods big enough to hold someone twice my size if necessary.

Inside one of them was Smorkus Flinders.

I had been eager to unfreeze him, because while I was fighting him in Dimension X, our vanished friend Snout had mysteriously managed to whisper in my head that Smorkus Flinders knew something about where my father was.

I had gone berserk then, and tried to pound the information out of him. But all he would say was that BKR knew something about it. Now BKR was missing. But it was clear Smorkus Flinders knew something about him.

And BKR seemed to be at the root of all this.

It was time to see what we could find out.

We had shrunk the monster, of course. Otherwise there was no way we could have fit him in the ship. (At his regular size he was so huge he could stick me in his ear—I know, because he did it once.)

Now, even though at full size I'm half again as tall as the crew, when we shrink they make us all the same size: about two inches.

We had tried to bring Smorkus Flinders down to that size as well. But he was normally so enormous we could only manage to get him down to four inches, which meant that though he was vastly tiny for him, he was still twice the height of the rest of us.

Despite that, I had an urge to say, "Not so big now, are you tough guy?" when we pulled him out of the pod.

I resisted, for two reasons: (1) Tar Gibbons has taught me that true warriors are gracious in victory; and (2) I was afraid if I made him mad he might not tell us what we wanted to know.

Being small didn't make Smorkus Flinders any more pleasant to look at. He had rough orange skin, a mouthful of jagged green teeth, and a nose that resembled a tree trunk with four major roots. But it wasn't those strangenesses that made him so ugly. (Heck, some of my friends on the *Ferkel* were at least as weird.) It was his *attitude*—the anger that seemed to flow like a solid wave from his smoldering green eyes—that gave me the creeps.

Some of that anger was for the world in general. But right now a lot of it was directed at me in particular, since I was the one who had defeated him while we were in Dimension X.

Later I noticed him glaring at Grakker as well, and remembered that back when we were in Dimension X, Snout had mentioned the captain offending Smorkus Flinders so greatly that the monster was thirsty for revenge. I wondered once more what that was all about.

Glowing blue rings surrounded the monster's neck, his waist, his wrists, and his ankles. These were what kept him from attacking us, or just running off.

Using a control box that connected to the blue rings, the Tar and I led the monster back to the conference room, then took our places at the table. Grakker and Madame Pong were still there, but Phil had had to go back to the bridge, to take the ship through a tricky passage.

Madame Pong led the interrogation, which she started by asking the monster his name. Since we already knew this, I figured it was some kind of formality.

Even though we already knew the answer, Smorkus Flinders had no intention of cooperating. He just glared at us, his lips clamped together tighter than a clam's shell.

Madame Pong repeated the question.

Smorkus Flinders continued to glare.

"You know, we can compel you to answer," said Madame Pong softly.

Still the monster remained silent.

Madame Pong closed her eyes, a gesture I had come to recognize as something like a sigh. Without opening them, she said, "Rod, go ask Phil for a truth helmet."

I started to ask what a truth helmet was, caught the look on Grakker's face, and decided to do as ordered. With the chibling clinging to my shoulder, I went to fetch the helmet.

When I told Phil what I had come for, he shifted several of his leaves, making the slightest rustling sound. Suddenly a whiz of blue fur shot past me. I jumped in surprise, then realized he had sent Plink to do the job.

Plink was Phil's symbiotic companion, a little creature who fetched and carried for him. In return, Plink got to eat any branches, leaves, and nuts Phil was done with. I had never figured out exactly how Phil and Plink communicated. Now I wondered if the rustling leaves were part of how they "talked."

Before I could ask, Plink came skittling back, carrying something that looked like a basketball that had been painted black, then sliced in half. Phil stretched out a tendril, took the helmet from Plink, and passed it to me.

I reached out to pet Plink, but he made a little squeak, then jumped up and disappeared behind Phil's leaves.

"He's a one-plant sort of creature," burped Phil apologetically.

I nodded. It wasn't like I needed another furry friend, since I could hardly go anywhere without the chibling. But having little animals around made me feel more at home.

"Thanks," I said, and took the helmet back to the interrogation room.

"Place it on him," said Grakker when I walked through the door.

I had to use a chair to get high enough to put the helmet on the monster's head. As soon as I had it in place it began to vibrate and make a slight, high-pitched humming sound.

"What is your name?" asked Madame Pong yet again.

This time the monster answered without hesitation. "I am Smorkus Flinders."

They were the first words I had heard him speak since we had shrunk him. It was strange to hear his voice sound like something other than a cannon.

"Where are you from?" continued Madame Pong.

"The Valley of the Monsters, in Dimension X."

"Why did you kidnap Rod and Elspeth to your dimension?"

"To use them as bait."

"For what?"

"I wanted to capture Grakker."

"Why?"

He smiled. "You know."

The statement was true, but not useful. I knew that trick pretty well myself. But then, I could almost sympathize with Smorkus Flinders at the moment. Having to wear a helmet that made you tell the truth struck me as being a lot like living with my mother.

Madame Pong frowned. Clearly she was going to have to phrase her questions carefully to get information out of the monster.

"How did you know where to find Rod?"

"BKR told me."

That made me shiver, but Madame Pong nodded serenely and said, "Exactly what is your relationship to BKR?"

"Friend."

"Do you have other friends?"

"No."

"Why is BKR your friend?"

"We have a common goal."

"What is that?"

Smorkus Flinders smiled, showing a mouthful of craggy green teeth. With genuine pride he said, "We're going to destroy the universe."

"They're mad," snorted Grakker. "Both of them. Or one is mad and the other is a fool."

Tar Gibbons frowned. "Perhaps not." Leaning forward, it asked, "Do you actually have a way to commit this horrible crime?"

Smorkus Flinders's smile grew even broader.

"We're building a time bomb. All we need to finish it is Rod Allbright's—"

Before he could finish the sentence, he gasped and began to make a strangled noise. His eyes rolled back in his head. He shuddered violently, then toppled with a crash, landing flat on his back.

CHAPTER 6

Chibling Rivalry

"ROD ALLBRIGHT'S *WHAT?*" I CRIED, STARTING toward the monster. "What do I have that you need?"

"Freeze right there, Deputy Allbright!" barked Grakker.

I couldn't figure out why, until I realized he was concerned that Smorkus Flinders might be trying to pull some trick. Then I was embarrassed. If Smorkus Flinders had somehow managed to break the control of the blue rings and was faking his distress, he would have had me as a prisoner—and bargaining piece—for sure.

But he wasn't faking, and as it turned out, nothing we tried could rouse him from his stupor.

"His vital signs are solid," said Madame Pong after a thorough examination. "Physically, he is alive and well. Mentally, he is totally nonresponsive."

"We had a kid like that in fifth grade," I said.

Despite the wisecrack my voice was bitter, and I was only joking to keep from screaming. Smorkus Flinders was supposed to know something about what had happened to my father, and I had been aching to find out what that might be. But instead of getting a chance to ask him, I had just been handed another mystery.

"What happened to him?" asked Grakker impatiently.

Blinking its big eyes, Tar Gibbons said, "I suspect BKR has done something to keep him from revealing their plans."

"BKR isn't here," I said, pointing out the obvious.

"Two things are possible," replied the Tar. It blinked again, then said, "Actually, more things are possible than we can imagine. However, two things come to mind at the moment. The first is that BKR set some trigger in Smorkus Flinders's head to shut him down should he come too close to revealing their plans."

"What's the second possibility?" I asked, feeling my own head nervously.

"That BKR has a mental connection to Smorkus Flinders and was monitoring the conversation. When we got too close to information he wanted kept secret, he did this."

"Wouldn't he have to be awfully close to us

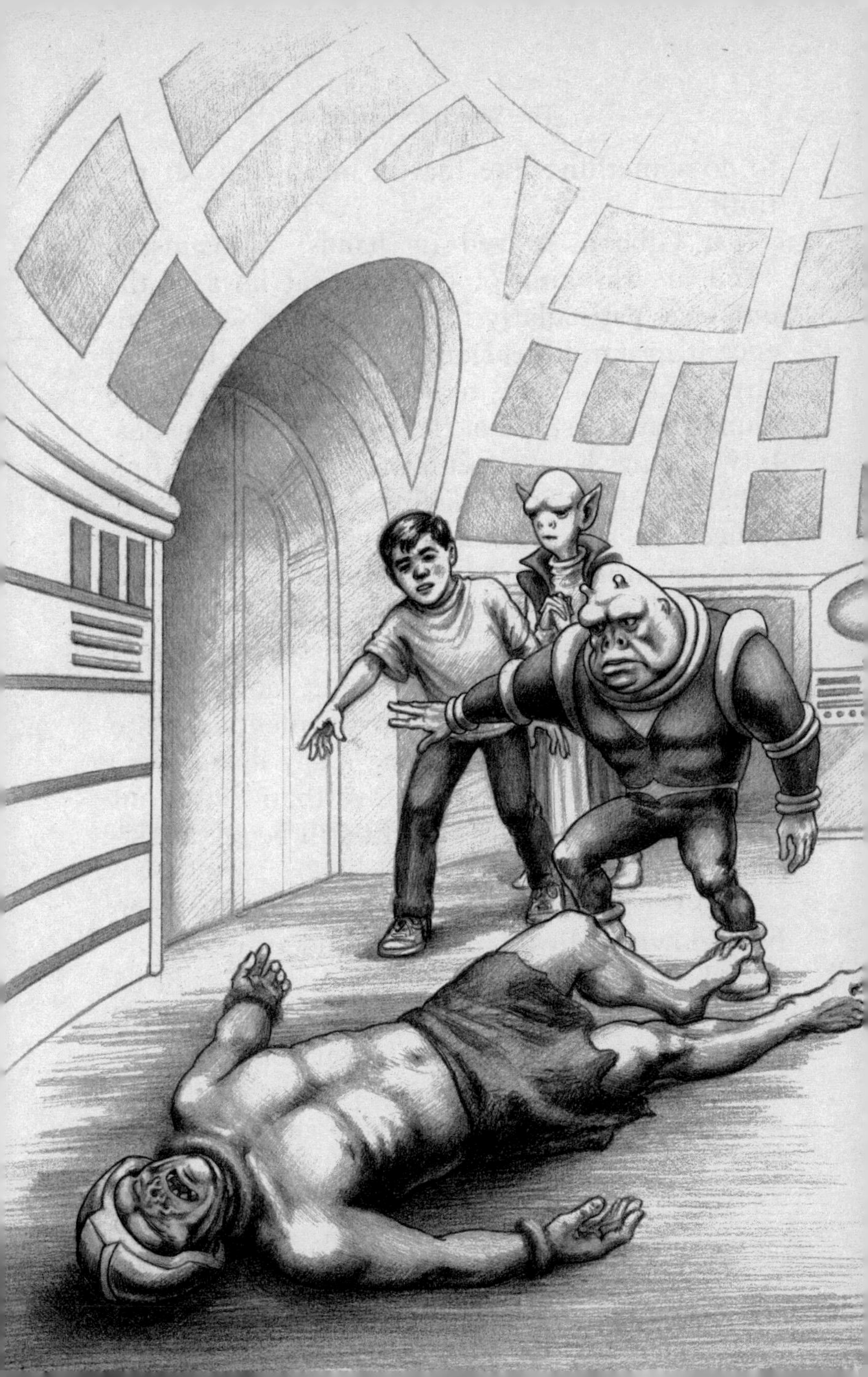

to do something like that? I mean, look at the timing—"

Tar Gibbons waved its hands in dismissal. "You are thinking of the physical laws of the universe, particularly the universe as we experience it in our dimension. But while the limit on physical speed seems to be that of light, we have found that the speed of *thought* is instantaneous. If two beings have a mental connection, that link defies distance. The thoughts of one can be experienced by the other at the very moment they occur, even if the two beings are at opposite ends of the galaxy."

"In which case, it may be just as well that Smorkus Flinders has been shut down," said Grakker. "If he really does have a mental link to BKR, it would be like having a spy device here on the ship. Wouldn't BKR love that! Better put him back in storage. He might still be broadcasting, despite his condition."

Grakker thought about this for a moment, then bent down, rolled Smorkus Flinders over, and yelled into his ear, "Are you listening, BKR? Well, now hear this! I stopped you once and I'll stop you again. You got that, you obnoxious little booger?"

Standing again, he said, "Now get him out of here."

* * *

"What do we do now?" I asked when Tar Gibbons and I had returned from putting Smorkus Flinders in cold storage. My stomach was churning with frustration, and I wondered how I would ever find out what had happened to my father.

"We contact Galactic Headquarters and tell them what has happened," replied Grakker. "We also continue to make full speed for Zambreno to see if we can pick up any trace of the *Merkel.* Until then the crew will continue in their regular duties. Deputy Allbright, I want you to assist Phil. It would be a good idea for you to begin getting familiar with the ship and how it operates."

Which was how I ended up on the bridge of the *Ferkel,* handing spare parts to a potted plant while it tried to reassemble a computer.

"Do you have a library?" Phil asked as we worked.

"Well, I've got a lot of books at home." I was trying to catch a glimpse of Plink, whom I could hear climbing around under Phil's leaves.

Phil lifted his orange and yellow blossom slightly, but not enough to let me see behind the petals. "Perhaps I should rephrase that. Do you have one of *our* books?"

"I have the one Snout gave me. I picked it up at home before we left." As always, when I spoke of our missing friend, I felt a pang of sorrow and wondered what had happened to him when he faded away in Dimension X.

Phil curled a tendril in annoyance. "No," he burped. "I mean a *total* book."

"I'm not sure I understand."

"Then you probably don't have one. But you should, and since I am in charge of ship's supplies, I'll provide you with one." He waved a tendril at the parts we were working with and said, "For one thing, it will help you with this stuff. Just a minute, I'll have Plink fetch one for you."

He rustled his leaves, and a blue blur shot out from underneath them.

A few minutes later Plink returned with a book-shaped object slightly larger than a typical paperback. Actually, since I was only two inches tall myself at the moment, it would be more accurate to say that it was the size a paperback *would* be if it had been shrunk down with me.

Anyway, it was pretty big for Plink, which slowed him down enough to give me a chance to get a better look at him. He had a long tube of a nose, but no tail or ears. His six legs—or four legs and two arms, depending on how you looked at them—appeared to be made out of fuzzy pipe cleaners bent to make knees, then bent again to make his long feet.

The chibling had been sitting on my shoulder

making a contented bubbling noise. Suddenly I felt it tighten its grip on my neck. Figuring this was a jealous reaction to the fact that I was paying attention to Plink, I reached up and stroked it, to reassure it that I was not thinking of replacing it. Meanwhile, I continued to study Plink, who had stopped too far away for me to be able to take the book from him.

Phil made a sound with his leaves. Plink didn't move.

Phil made the sound again.

Slowly Plink walked toward me, holding the book before it.

I reached out to take it.

Before I could close my fingers over the book, the chibling hurtled down my arm and launched itself at Plink. The little blue animal shrieked and tried to back away. It was too late. My sweet chibling had fastened on to Plink and, as near as I could tell, was doing its best to kill him.

Phil flapped his leaves helplessly, burping, "Stop them! Stop them! Stop them!"

I wanted to. But the two little animals were scratching and biting so fast and furiously that I couldn't keep track of which was where, much less figure out how to grab one of them.

Finally Phil managed to wrap a few tendrils around Plink. He tried to pry him out of the chibling's grasp, but Plink was enraged now, too, and totally unwilling to let go. Phil fired the rockets on the bottom of his pot and tried flying backward. All he managed to do was pull the snarling, snapping mass of blue and purple fur across the table.

Suddenly I knew what to do.

"I'm getting out of here!" I shouted, and sprinted out of the room.

I wasn't abandoning Phil. I was trying to take advantage of the chibling's desperate need to be with me.

It worked. The moment the creature realized I was leaving, it switched out of attack mode and tried to run off to join me.

Unfortunately, by now Plink was too enraged to just let go, so it took another moment or two for the chibling to squirm loose. Even then it only managed to break free because Phil was working so hard to keep his symbiote under control.

When the chibling finally came scurrying out to join me, it wrapped itself around my leg, chittering desperately—as if it hadn't been the one to start the whole problem!

To keep the chibling and Plink apart, I spent what was left of the day with Madame Pong, trying to program the ship's food system to provide stuff I could eat. I would describe something—

peanut butter, for example—and she would try to get the system to create it.

Texture and color were easy.

Taste, unfortunately, was something else altogether.

"If we could have brought a variety of foods from your home, the machine could just do a molecular analysis, and then turn out as much of it as you needed," muttered Madame Pong. "Too bad we had to leave in such a hurry."

I had to agree with her, especially after I sampled the ship's first attempt at chocolate chips. They tasted like a combination of chicken, blueberries, and earwax. (I'm just guessing about the last part; I never actually tasted earwax. But this stuff had a bizarre and horrible undertaste, and that's as good a way to describe it as any.)

The good news was, I could keep adjusting the stuff to try to get the taste right.

The bad news was, that was harder than you can imagine.

Madame Pong suggested I should also start sampling alien food to see what I might like from that. "But first we'll need to do a biological workup, to see what you can actually digest."

This eating business was more complicated than I had expected. I began to wish we could just stop at an interstellar McDonald's. I would have traded a year of my life for some french fries.

By the time the ship signaled it was time for some of us to rest, I was totally exhausted. Dragging into my room, I stared eagerly at my antigravity bed. I couldn't wait to climb into it and float my way to sleep.

But before I could get out of my clothes, I heard a banging on the inside wall of my storage closet.

"Rod!" called a familiar voice. "Rod, let me out!"

CHAPTER 7

Crime and Punishment

IT WAS ELSPETH, OF COURSE.

"What are you doing here?" I cried when I opened the closet. "You're supposed to be back on Earth, with Mom!"

Ignoring the question, she said, "I can't believe you were going to go without me, Rod!"—as if *I* were the one who had done something wrong!

"Elspeth, this isn't a vacation. It's a life-and-death mission."

"Yeah, and I plan to be part of it."

"Grakker isn't going to like this."

"Grakker doesn't like anything. And I'd rather be in trouble than be left behind."

I sighed. "Well, you asked for it. We'd better go let them know you're here."

"You don't have to tell him right away. Let's keep it a secret for a while."

"Elspeth, I can't keep you a secret. I'm an official deputy. For all I know they might kick me off the Galactic Patrol if I don't tell them you're here. And that would mean I couldn't go look for Dad."

She frowned. "Do you think Grakker will be mad?"

"He's always mad. For this, I'd say he'll be somewhere between volcanic and nuclear."

She leaned back into the storage space. "Then I'm going to stay here for a while."

"He'll just come and get you."

"Don't tell him where I am!"

"Elspeth, I can barely tell a lie when the fate of the world is at stake. I'm not about to tell one just because you don't want to get in trouble. Besides, you being here sure wasn't my idea! If you had asked me, I would have told you to forget it. You're going to have to face Grakker sooner or later. Let's get it over with."

Muttering darkly, she climbed out of the storage space. I almost felt sorry for her—until I reminded myself that this was entirely her own doing.

I was used to Grakker being cranky, but even I was surprised at how furious he was over what Elspeth had done.

After I brought her to the bridge, he called the entire crew—except Phil, who stayed on duty to pilot the ship through a tricky dimension—back to the conference room.

Madame Pong asked him to wait for a minute before he started to speak. Stepping behind him, she pulled something about the size of a half-used pencil from the back of his head. Then she took another, similar object from the pocket of her robe and inserted it in place of the first one.

"Judicial module," she whispered as she took her place next to me.

Indeed, Grakker was surprisingly calm when he spoke. However, he was also *very* serious. Reading from a screen embedded in the table in front of him, he said sternly, "Elspeth McMasters, you are in violation of Galactic Ordinance Number 176.43.981. Also Galactic Ordinance Number 865.221.1, Galactic Ordinance Number 99.418.72, and Galactic Ordinance Number 6. Do you have anything to say in your own defense?"

Knowing Elspeth, I had figured she was going to try to cute her way out of this mess, and I was right. She twirled her hair, smiled her "I'm so cute you can't possibly stay mad at me" smile, and said, "I'm sorry. I just got carried away because I wanted to be with you guys so much."

I'd seen her do this kind of thing to her father a hundred times, and it always worked, which was probably one reason she was such a brat.

Unfortunately for Elspeth, Grakker was immune to cuteness.

When he began to growl, Elspeth switched tactics. Putting her hands on her hips, she said, "I also came along because it wasn't fair that Rod should get to have all the adventures."

"Fair is not the issue," replied Grakker sharply.

"Well, it should be!"

Grakker stood up. "Guilty as charged. Because we cannot turn back, we will have to deal with your flagrant violations within the confines of this vessel, and in keeping with its ongoing mission."

"Why can't we turn back?" asked Elspeth. "We haven't been gone that long. Just turn the ship around."

She looked a little nervous, and I got the impression she was finally starting to realize how much trouble she was in.

Grakker twitched, as if the judicial module was struggling to keep his natural crankiness in check. "Time is only part of the matter—though we certainly have none to waste on your foolishness, since the clues to what BKR is up to could well vanish while we were engaged in the fool's mission of taking you back. However, the main issue is energy."

I remembered a conversation during our first

adventure when the aliens had told me that they used "energy credits" the way we use money.

Locking his fingers in front of him, Grakker said solemnly, "To take you back now would require more energy than this entire crew earns in a year. Because such a trip would not be an authorized expense, that energy use would come out of our pay. And I am not going to sacrifice a full year's wages for everyone on this ship simply because *you* wanted to have a little adventure!"

Elspeth turned pale. I actually felt sorry for her; I'm sure that until that very moment she had figured if she got caught and the aliens were too mad, they would just turn around and take her back.

At the same time another part of my mind was wondering if I would be getting paid, too. After all, I was an official deputy. The thought was kind of cool. How many energy credits did a deputy get? What could you spend them on?

My selfish thoughts were interrupted by Elspeth saying, "Then just let me join the crew. If Rod can, I can."

"I am not going to *reward* you for stowing away!" snapped Grakker. "I'm afraid I will have to keep you in suspense."

"You mean you're not going to tell me what you're going to do to me?" asked Elspeth nervously.

Grakker looked confused. "I just told you: I'm going to keep you in suspense."

"I'm in suspense now!"

"Excuse me," said Madame Pong. Stepping behind Grakker, she gave him a solid whack on the side of the head.

"Problems with the language implant," she said, returning to her seat. "Try again, Captain."

Grakker's nostrils twitched, but he said nothing to Madame Pong. Turning back to Elspeth, he said, "I am going to put you in suspended animation."

"You mean you're going to freeze me like a bag of peas? Rod, you can't let them do this to me!"

Right, I thought. *You get yourself into this mess by doing something you know I would tell you not to, and then you expect* me *to get you out.*

But she was my cousin. So I took a deep breath and said, "Captain, couldn't we—"

"Silence, Deputy Allbright!"

"Yes, sir," I said meekly.

"You will not be frozen like a . . . a bag of peas," said Grakker. "Whatever they are. You will be placed in a special chamber where your life functions will be put on hold, just like any other prisoner of the Galactic Patrol. It will not hurt. It will not damage you. It will simply keep you out of my hair for a while."

(Another little glitch in the language implant; Grakker didn't have any hair to keep out of.)

I turned to Madame Pong. "Can't *you* do something about this?" I whispered.

She put her long hands palm out, in a sign of negation. "The captain is in control on the ship, Rod. Moreover, I agree with his judgment. Elspeth made a reckless and dangerous decision, and she must pay for it. However, no harm will come to her. In fact, this is actually the most merciful thing the captain can do. The Space Code does allow for much more severe penalties."

"Like what?"

She made an expression of distaste. "We could jettison her."

"Dump her into space?" I yelped, earning myself an angry look from Grakker and a shriek of horror from Elspeth. Lowering my voice, I added, "I thought cruelty was considered the greatest crime in the civilized galaxy."

"Cruelty is the needless inflicting of pain. Justice, however, requires that people be held responsible for their own actions—and their consequences. A ship is not like a country, Rod. We are traveling through a vast emptiness in a tiny, fragile shell."

I wasn't sure that all made sense to me. *Oh, well,* I thought. *They're aliens. Not everything they think is going to make sense to you.* Then

I remembered that I was part alien myself, and felt really confused.

Grakker pronounced sentence. "Tar Gibbons, I want you and Deputy Allbright to put Elspeth in a Sus-An Pod. Set the release time for one week from now. We will check on her then, and refreeze her as necessary until we can decide what to do with her."

My stomach twisted. Angry as I was with Elspeth for stowing away, I didn't think I could bring myself to be the one who actually put her in cold storage.

If I refused, what would they do? Kick me off the Galactic Patrol?

Put me in cold storage myself?

Jettison me?

Elspeth was staring at me, her eyes desperate.

She looks a lot like her mother, who happens to look a lot like my mother. (They are sisters, after all.)

When you get right down to it, Elspeth looks a lot like my mother—not to mention something like Thing One and Thing Two.

Please, Rod, she said, mouthing the words without really speaking them aloud.

With a sigh I turned to Grakker. "I'm sorry, Captain, but I can't do this."

If Madame Pong hadn't installed that judicial module in the captain's head, this might have been the end of my career with the Galactic Patrol. But the seconds Grakker spent struggling between whether to remain calm or to explode at my defiance were enough for Madame Pong to race to his side.

She had a quick, hurried conference with him, carried out in urgent whispers. Though I couldn't hear all of it, I did catch several phrases—mostly when Grakker repeated something Madame Pong had said. These included "untrained deputy," "primitive planet," and "highly structured rules of kinship."

These last words in particular seemed to get Grakker's attention. He sat back in his chair, tweaked his nubby horns a couple of times, then nodded. Turning to me, he said, "Deputy Allbright, in view of your inexperience and cultural conditioning, you are excused in this matter. Madame Pong and Tar Gibbons will escort the stowaway to her storage location."

I was relieved that I didn't have to freeze Elspeth myself. Even so, I wondered if I should try harder to prevent it from happening.

I started to speak up, but Madame Pong caught my eye and shook her head.

"Take her away," said Grakker.

"NOOOOO!" shrieked Elspeth. "NO! NO! NO! NO! NO! Rod, don't let them do this to me!"

I didn't really have any say in the matter. So I did the only thing I could think of. Turning to Grakker, I said, "Captain, I volunteer to be frozen first, in order to show the stowaway that it is safe."

Elspeth stopped screaming and looked at me in astonishment.

Madame Pong looked pleased, if a little surprised.

Grakker sighed. "If you must, Deputy Allbright."

I sighed, too. "I must."

Standing beside my cousin, I went off to be frozen like a bag of peas.

As it turned out, it was a darn good thing that I did.

CHAPTER 8

A Voice from Beyond

I STOOD BESIDE A SUSPENDED ANIMATION POD AND thought, *Me and my big mouth.*

It wasn't that I was afraid of going into it, exactly. In my head, I was sure that it would be no problem at all. But something in my gut was squirming in horror, shouting "NO! NO! NO! NO! NO!" just the way Elspeth had.

But it was too late to turn back. Taking a deep breath, I turned to Elspeth and said, "You'll see—it's no big deal."

"Are you going to stay under for as long as I do?" she asked.

I rolled my eyes. "Of course not! I'm just showing you that it's safe."

With the chibling clinging to my leg, I climbed into the pod. Then I leaned back into the cushions and waited for Tar Gibbons to close the lid over me.

"We've set this for eight hours," whispered the Tar. "Since it was time to sleep anyway, you might as well get a good night's rest out of it. I will see you in the morning, my krevlik."

"See you then," I replied.

When I had seen units like this in movies, they usually had glass lids—I suppose because they look more cool that way. But these pods were built to use, not to look pretty, and they had solid covers. When the Tar closed the lid, I was plunged into utter blackness.

I felt a surge of panic. I didn't want to be frozen!

I heard a hiss of gas.

Within a minute I began to drift into a strange, dark sleep.

Suspended animation is weird. It's a time without time, a constant *now*—a single, endless moment marked only by the changing of your dreams.

No telling how many dreams, no telling how long they last.

I dreamed of my mother; heard her calling me, sensed her worrying about me. I tried to answer her, but couldn't.

I dreamed about the twins, about playing in

the yard with them, about bopping them good night with their teddy bears.

I dreamed about my father, reliving the wild and windy October night he had helped me carve a jack-o'-lantern, then said, "I'm going out for a walk, I'll be back in a while," and disappeared from our lives.

I don't know how many times I dreamed *that* scene.

Counting wasn't an option.

No time passed.

All time passed.

I floated, not really aware of anything, yet somehow knowing I existed. According to what Phil told me later, even though your body processes are brought to a virtual stop, somehow your brain doesn't stop working.

Just as well, I suppose.

If it had, I couldn't have gotten the message that gave us a shot at saving the universe.

It started with someone calling my name.

Rod. Rod, can you hear me?

It took me a while to realize this wasn't just another phantom of my frozen mind. It was actually someone trying to get through to me.

It took me even longer to realize who it was.

Snout! Is that you?

Yes. At least, I think it's me. He sounded puzzled. *Actually, I'm, not really sure.*

Where are you?

Everywhere?

I wasn't sure if he was asking me or telling me. Suddenly vast wonder, joy, and terror swept through me. A million voices seemed to sing in my head. I thought Snout was weeping.

Before I could figure any of this out, the pod began to wake me up.

For a few minutes I floated in a pleasant kind of half-sleep, my memories of the beautiful and horrifying connection with Snout drifting away like fragments of a dream when an alarm clock goes off. Then I started coming out of suspended animation fairly fast and the memories vanished altogether as life surged back into my arms and legs. "Yow!" I cried as my entire body began tingling the way your foot does when you sit on it the wrong way and it goes to sleep.

A moment later Tar Gibbons opened the lid of the Sus-An Pod.

"How long was I under?" I asked.

"Only for the night," replied the Tar as it helped me out of the pod. "Just as I promised."

"Where's Elspeth?"

The Tar pointed to the pod next to me.

I placed my hand gently on the sealed green

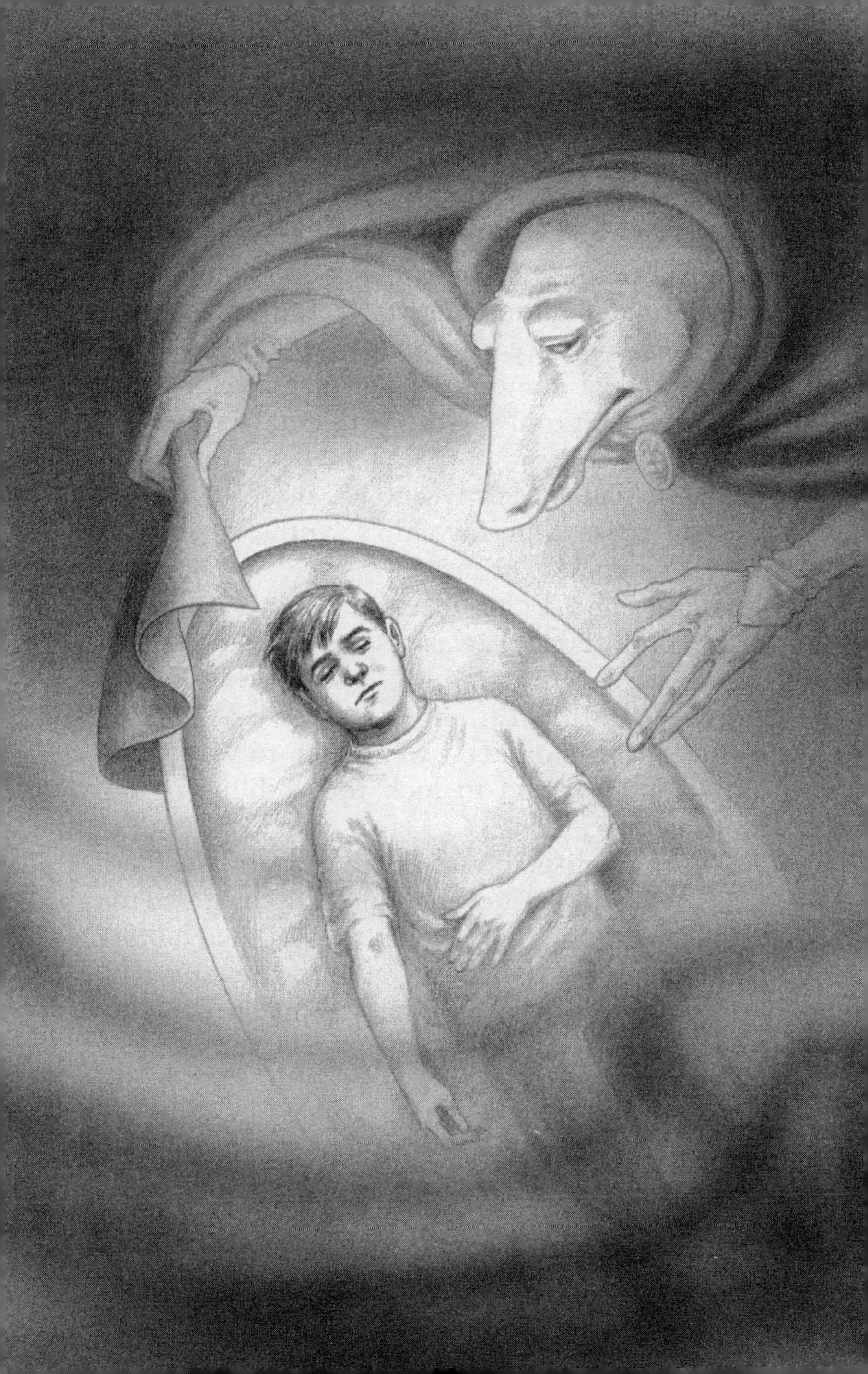

lid. "See you later, Cousin," I said, feeling oddly lonely.

After breakfast Tar Gibbons helped me choose a uniform. As a mere deputy in the Galactic Patrol, I had a choice of three simple outfits, all of which looked something like green versions of Grakker's suit, only without the extra rings and stuff.

Once I had made my choice, the Tar showed me how to program the ship's synthesizer to run out a few copies for me.

The uniform I chose turned out to be surprisingly comfortable. It was also easy to move in—important for my training sessions in Warrior Science with the Tar.

At Grakker's orders, I went back to work with Phil—though I had to lock the chibling in my room before I did.

It *eeeped* miserably at being left behind.

Though Plink was even more skittish around me than before, Phil didn't seem to hold the chibling incident against me. In fact, after the next meal he came to my room with the book he had been trying to give me earlier. I apologized over and over for what had happened to Plink. Finally Phil waved his tendrils and burped, "Enough! Here, take this. I think you will find it useful."

I turned the book over a couple of times, but

couldn't manage to open it until Phil showed me how.

It had a single page, which turned out to be what we would call a viewscreen—except it was so smooth and easy to read you would have thought it was really good paper. On the side of the book were dials and buttons you could use to change the way the words looked—to make them bigger or smaller, lighter or darker.

When Phil showed me how to find things in the book, I realized he was right; it really was like a whole library, since it contained as much information as about twenty thousand books.

A lot of it was nonfiction, of course—it was crammed with all sorts of reference books. Given the fact that I knew almost nothing about the world beyond Earth, this was going to be very useful. But I was even more excited about the fact that the book held thousands of *stories*: novels, epics, even collections of myths, legends, and fairy tales from planets all over the galaxy.

"How do they fit it all in here?" I asked, looking at the book in amazement.

"Computer stuff," burped Phil. "You're not that far from being able to do things like this on Earth."

"How do you know *that?*" I asked uneasily.

"We monitor your technology. Just to be safe."

* * *

It wasn't until I was drifting off to sleep that night—back in that half-asleep, half-awake condition—that I remembered my conversation with Snout.

Surely it had been a dream.

And yet.

And yet . . .

I hesitated for a long time, then decided I had better tell someone about it. With the chibling wrapped around my lcg, I went to look for one of the crew members.

I met Madame Pong as she was leaving the recreation room. I told her what had disturbed me, feeling a little silly now that I was saying it out loud. But she took what I had to say very seriously.

When I asked her why, she said, "Remember, Rod, you have already been in contact with Snout once since his disappearance. So it seems possible—even likely—that he might contact you again. I suspect that your being in suspended animation made it easier for him to do so, since it would eliminate all outside distractions and let you 'hear' something that might normally fall beneath your level of perception."

We went to find Grakker. When I told him my story I could tell what he had in mind just by the way he looked at me.

"Oh, no," I said. "I don't want to go back in one of those pods!"

"I would do it myself," said Grakker gruffly, "had Snout seen fit to contact *me* instead of you."

I started to say something, then stopped when I had the astonishing realization that Grakker was jealous! I decided to *keep* my mouth shut—a feat made easier by the fact that I had no idea what to say.

"Tonight you will sleep in a Sus-An Pod again," said Grakker. "Tomorrow we will wake you more slowly than we did this time, with the hope that you will have a better memory of anything Snout might say to you if he makes contact again."

So I spent another night in the pod.

Since time has no meaning when you are in suspended animation, I have no way of telling exactly *when* it was that Snout came to me.

But he did.

His message this time was short, but so sharp and desperate that it burned itself into my brain. It didn't make any difference whether they woke me fast or slowly the next morning, there was no way I was going to forget it.

BKR has deceived you. Do not go to Zambreno, it will only waste your time. Go to the

Mentat instead. You must go to the Mentat. The fate of the universe depends on it!

He repeated the message three times.

What do we do when we get there? I thought desperately.

Someone will help you.

Then, briefly, I felt a surge of despair, and received one final message.

Tell Grakker that I am a prisoner of the Ferkada. Ask him to find me, and free me.

CHAPTER 9

Renegades of the Galaxy

WHEN THE POD OPENED THE NEXT MORNING, I FOUND the entire crew waiting for me.

"Well?" asked Grakker eagerly, before I even got out. "Did you get a message from Snout?"

I nodded.

"What did he tell you?"

I repeated Snout's messages exactly—the one about going to the Mentat, and the one about him being a prisoner of the Ferkada.

Grakker looked at me in astonishment and horror. "Are you absolutely sure that's what he said?"

"He repeated the part about going to the Mentat three times."

Grakker turned to Madame Pong and Tar Gibbons. "Do you think this is genuine? Is it possible Deputy Allbright is hallucinating?"

I blinked in surprise. Though I was sure that

the messages were not merely dreams, it had never occurred to me that I might have hallucinated them.

Madame Pong looked troubled. "Given the message that Rod got from Snout while we were in Dimension X, I would tend to think that this is also real."

Tar Gibbons blinked its big eyes and added, "Of course, *that* message could have been a hallucination as well. One can never be sure with these things."

Grakker turned back to me. "Think carefully, Deputy Allbright. Did Snout say *anything* else—anything that might prove this message is genuine?"

I shook my head.

He muttered under his breath and stomped out of the room.

"Why is he so upset?" I asked.

Madame Pong looked grim. "We face a difficult choice. Do we continue toward Zambreno, as originally planned—or do we divert our course and head for the Mentat? If we choose wrong, BKR wins, and millions will weep.

"This decision would be difficult under the best of circumstances. But it is made more complicated for the captain because while he does not think highly of the Mentat, right now it is his greatest desire to go there."

I started to ask why, then realized the answer on my own.

Snout had told me he was being held prisoner by "the Ferkada." But Madame Pong had not been able to find any solid mention of this name in the ship's data base. Our only clue had come from the Ting Wongovia, a Mental Master we had met in Dimension X. He had told us that to find out about the Ferkada we would have to visit the Mentat.

Of course Grakker wanted to go to the Mentat! But he had been ordered to continue with our first mission, which had to do with finding my father. Had he hoped to combine that mission with a search for the missing Snout? If so, the message we got ordering us to go to Zambreno had ruined any chance for that.

Now I was giving him a reason to disobey those orders. But how could he think clearly about it, when it was what he wanted to do anyway?

For the first time I felt sorry for Grakker.

"Think, Rod," said Madame Pong. "Was there anything in either of the messages you got that could *prove* it was from Snout?"

"Or anything that might prove it *wasn't* real?" added Tar Gibbons, reaching into the Sus-An pod to help me out. "Anything that might indicate, for example, that it came from your own subconscious?"

"Or even, somehow, from BKR?" burped Phil,

wrapping a tendril around my right arm to steady me while I waited for my legs to stop tingling.

I thought about their questions, then said, "All I can tell you is that it *felt* like Snout."

Madame Pong sighed. "That's a good answer, but not totally useful. The messages could feel like Snout because they *are* from Snout, or simply because when Snout did the training transfer that taught you how to use your flying belt, it left enough of an impression in your mind for it to recreate the feel of him in a dream."

"So there's no way of knowing if these messages are real?" I asked nervously.

Madame Pong shook her head. "No way at all. Which does not change the fact that we are going to have to make a decision about them."

Grakker came storming back into the room. "I have spoken with the command center. They ordered us to continue toward Zambreno as originally scheduled."

I gasped. "We can't do that!" I cried. I stopped, surprised at how strongly I felt.

Grakker gave me the fiercest of the many fierce looks that he had given me since I first met him. "How certain of that are you, Deputy Allbright? Before you answer, understand this: I believe that BKR is planning something horrible beyond belief, something that must be prevented at all costs. If we make the wrong choice—if we go to the Mentat when we should go to Zambreno, or vice versa—we may lose our only chance to prevent some hideously cruel crime.

"Know this as well: If we need to go to the Mentat, then that is the course I will choose, in defiance of orders from headquarters."

I saw Madame Pong flinch slightly. "Do you know what that means, Rod?" she asked.

"Not really," I whispered. I was getting a bad feeling about this.

Grakker's nostrils flared. "It means that I will no longer be a legitimate captain. It also means that the crew—including you—will have to make decisions of your own. You can accept my orders, in which case you will become, like me, renegades. Or you can band together to overthrow my command, which will be mutiny, but will almost certainly be supported by any court. Or one or all of you can legitimately ask to abandon ship. I will not stand in the way of anyone who wants to use one of our small life vessels. They will easily take you to a safe haven.

"Be clear on this: If I go to the Mentat and you choose to stay with me as part of my crew, your public honor is sacrificed. The moment we make that choice, we will no longer be members of the Galactic Patrol. Every legitimate ship in the galaxy becomes our enemy. If we are caught, we will be tried and subject to the harshest of penalties."

"We can't make that kind of decision based only on what I experienced in suspended animation," I whispered in horror.

"I have no choice but to choose," said Grakker.

"Warrior Science teaches us that the most difficult thing to do is make decisions," murmured Tar Gibbons.

What neither the Tar nor Grakker said, but what I could not escape, was that the captain was going to have to base his decision mostly on how strongly I believed that what I had experienced in the Sus-An Pod was real.

Grakker turned to Phil. "Determine the swiftest route to the Mentat. See if it has any overlap with our present course. Let me know how much time we have before we would have to diverge."

"Aye-aye, Captain," said Phil. He lifted one of his leaves in salute, then fired up his pot and headed for the bridge.

"Maybe you'd better put me back in suspended animation," I said. "I might get another message from Snout."

"Wait until we get our report from Phil," said Grakker. "We may not have time for that."

Indeed, less than two minutes later Phil's voice came over the ship's speaker system. "Captain, the Zambreno system and the Mentat are in opposite directions. Even so, I have found one dimensional hop that will take us closer to both of them. After that, we have to go one way or the other."

"How long do we have?" growled Grakker.

"Forty-five minutes."

"Do you want me to go back into the pod?" I asked.

Grakker shook his head. "It takes longer than that simply to move you fully into suspended animation and bring you back out."

He turned to Madame Pong and Tar Gibbons. "I am going to my quarters. I will accept input and suggestions for the next twenty minutes. I will have my decision in the next thirty minutes. Please assemble the crew in the conference room at that time."

He turned and left the room.

"I'm sorry," I whispered. "I'm so sorry."

Tar Gibbons put a hand on my shoulder. "This is not a time to apologize. It is a time to think."

I was already thinking so hard I felt like my brain was going to explode. But try as I might, I could not find the tiniest bit of information that would tell me for certain whether or not the messages I had received were really from Snout.

Nothing other than the fact that I believed they were.

Thirty minutes later we gathered in the conference room.

Grakker looked around the table and said, "I have decided to take the ship to the Mentat. What say each of you?"

Tar Gibbons breathed a heavy sigh. Putting its hands on the table, it said, "Warrior Science teaches us that the approved path and the right path are not always one and the same. I will follow my captain, wherever he leads."

Grakker nodded and turned to Phil.

"I have to go along," said the plant gruffly. "You'd just get lost without me."

Again Grakker nodded. "Madame Pong?"

Her yellow face was more somber than I had ever seen it, and her eyes were like deep wells of grief. Her voice no more than a whisper, she said, "Though it cost me my life, my honor, and the respect of my family, I stand with my captain."

Grakker fixed his eyes on me. To my surprise, there was no hint of anger in them. He didn't say "This is all your fault" or "Look what you've gotten us into." He just waited for my decision, offering even me, even now, a chance to step aside from what I had started.

But there was no turning back.

"I stand with my captain," I said.

Grakker nodded. "Then it is decided. We are renegades. Let us pray that we have made the right decision."

CHAPTER 10

Up from the Worm Farm

THE TERRIBLE DECISION SEEMED TO BIND US TOGETHER in some way—and to loosen something in us as well.

Or maybe it was that we just needed to get rid of some tension.

Whatever the reason, that night we had a party in the recreation room which was one of the most hilarious things I have ever experienced. When Tar Gibbons got up and did a comic dance it had learned "back when I was a wee farfel," I ended up laughing so hard I nearly fell over.

Before the party was finished they even got me dancing, which is an all-time first, I want to tell you.

When I talked to the Tar about the party the next day, it told me, "A warrior's greatest battles are with itself. A clear decision is always a reason to rejoice."

* * *

According to Phil it would take us nearly a week to reach the Mentat. "Though it's a complicated question," he said, "since the answer depends on how you measure time. For example, the ship's cycle for a 'day' equals twenty-five hours and fifteen minutes of your time. This schedule is the best compromise for everyone on board—though it does not take into account *your* biorhythms, since we haven't put those into the computer yet. Nor does it include the fact that Snout is no longer with us. We should probably readjust it a bit when we get the chance.

"We are scheduled to reach Planet Mentat in 7.35 ship's days. That would be the same as 7.73 Earth days—assuming, of course, that none of the dimensional pathways have shifted. If that happens, then all bets are off."

So if nothing went wrong, it would take us slightly over a week, whether you counted by Earth time or ship's time. It was unbelievably frustrating to feel that what we were doing was so important, yet to know that nothing I could do would get us there one second faster.

We were traveling incredibly fast when you considered that we were going to end up thousands of light-years from where we started. Even so, I felt as if we were slouching along.

* * *

Despite the tension, I found myself falling into a steady routine.

In the morning I joined the crew for breakfast in the recreation room. This was always an exciting event, as I never knew what the others would be eating. Sometimes it was pretty revolting, especially since Tar Gibbons seemed to prefer its food to be alive until the very moment it popped it into its mouth.

After breakfast I would work in the control room with Phil, learning how to operate the ship. I was surprised they would let a kid learn this kind of stuff—and even more surprised (not to mention nervous) when Phil had me take control one day.

Tar Gibbons seemed surprised at my surprise. "If you don't learn real things, how will you ever cope in the real world?" it asked, blinking its big eyes. "By the way, I want you to meet me in the training room after lunch."

I liked training with the Tar. We started each session with a time of quiet sitting while we sought the Katsu Maranda—a state of joyful harmony with the universe. I couldn't always get there, but even trying seemed to improve my state of mind.

Then we moved into the physical section of the training, which I also enjoyed. This had been a surprise to me, since I had hated taking gym at home. Of course, that was partly because I was so clumsy that people were always laughing at me. But the Tar was patient and never laughed. Oddly, I found that the less I worried about screwing up, the less I actually did screw up. And when I did make mistakes, they weren't such a big deal.

The Tar's training sessions sometimes left me limp and lame. But I could feel myself continuing to get stronger and more coordinated, so I didn't really mind.

In the evening we would gather in the ship's recreation room—sometimes all of us, but more often without Grakker. Madame Pong liked to tell stories during that time. I was surprised that with all their incredible technology—three-dimensional movies you could play in the middle of the room, helmets that made you feel as if you were *inside* a game—that the aliens still liked to do something as simple as listen to stories.

"A living being can speak from the heart, Rod," said Madame Pong, when I asked her about it. "The connection is different than with an electronically told story, or even with a book. It is being to being—life to life."

Later, floating in my antigravity bed, I would spend a little while reading the book Phil had given me. Like Madame Pong's stories, it filled me with a great longing to see all the strange and wonderful places of the galaxy.

Despite the crew's friendliness, I was still homesick sometimes. I longed to see my mother, to play with the twins, to hear Bonehead's eager bark as he raced to greet me in the yard.

I was glad to have the chibling then, because it would cuddle up against me and make soothing sounds. It didn't solve the problem, but it did make me feel better.

A few times I even went to stand outside the pod where Elspeth was being kept in suspended animation, and talked to her as if she could hear me.

In some weird way this made me feel less alone.

The night before we were scheduled to arrive at Planet Mentat, Grakker *did* join Madame Pong, Phil, Tar Gibbons, and me in the recreation room.

Being so close to our goal seemed to put Grakker in a good mood. I decided to take advantage of this and see if I could get him to tell me some of the things I had been wondering about.

"Captain, when did you first meet BKR? How did you become such enemies?"

I figured if he answered at all, it would be some gruff comment that might give me a little more information. To my surprise, he said, "That's a good question, Deputy Allbright. I think it's time for you to know that story." He glanced at the others. "You know this tale already, of course. I will not be offended should you wish to leave."

"Not at all," murmured Madame Pong. "I enjoy your tales, Captain."

After we had all gotten some snacks and settled into our seats, Grakker went on.

"To understand the trouble with BKR and Smorkus Flinders, you have to know a little of my own history."

That was fine with me. I had been dying to learn more about the crew and where each of them came from.

"I was born on the planet Friskalama, on the farm run by my parents."

That was a surprise. I had always figured Grakker came from some super city. I would never have guessed he was a country kid, like me.

"What kind of farm was it?" I asked.

"Worm."

"Did people go fishing a lot on your planet?"

Grakker snorted. "Of course not. Worms are the primary source of meat on Friskalama. The ones my family raised were particularly large and tender."

"You *ate* them?" I cried.

Even before Grakker shot me the look of contempt that this question generated, I could have pulled out my tongue. I had been with the aliens long enough to know that the galaxy is wide and strange, and life goes on in all sorts of unexpected ways. And I had often watched Tar Gibbons devour the live snacks it raised in its own room.

I think the fact that Grakker looked more . . . well, more *human* than the Tar was part of what made his statement so shocking to me. That's really stupid, of course, since it would indicate I thought of the Tar as being *less* human, which was the farthest thing in the world from being the truth.

Grakker's response was swift and sharp. Fixing me with a level gaze, he said, "You should realize, Deputy Allbright, that most civilized beings refuse to eat animals as intelligent as the ones your people commonly raise for food."

One sentence and he managed to make me feel guilty for my entire planet's eating habits. I wondered if he and Mom had studied the same books on being in charge of people.

Madame Pong said gently, "And *you* must remember, Grakker, that Deputy Allbright still knows very little of the world beyond his planet. It would be best to excuse his ignorance and simply accept that for him to understand your story, he will need more details than you would ordinarily give."

Grakker looked at her for a moment, looked at me, glanced at the ceiling, grunted in disgust, then continued his story. Later I learned that the ship had recorded it and I could play it back anytime I wanted.

Here it is, word for word as he told it to me, including my questions and interruptions:

"I grew up on my parents' worm farm. My father, who loved what he did, had developed a brown and green striped worm that grew to the size of a man's arm and was particularly juicy and tasty. So we had many customers and were fairly well off as farm families go.

"As a boy I had to work in the worm pits, of course, which was only fair. But even as I stood knee deep in the smelly muck harvesting the worms, my heart was yearning for the stars. This was partly because my cousin Rakfratz was a member of the Galactic Patrol, and when he came to visit on holidays he would tell me fabulous stories of the distant worlds he had visited. I longed desperately to go to such places myself.

"I could read about them, of course—even experience them in our reality tank. But it wasn't the same as being there.

"I grew increasingly restless. Ma Grakker

would say, 'What's wrong, boy? You're as squirmy as a worm with intestinal blockage.' Of course, she had said this to me for as long as I could remember, but by the time I was eight years old—that would be about fourteen years by your planet's rotational system, Deputy Allbright—I found it a stupid and pointless thing to say.

"In their ninth year Friskan youths must take a Meditation Journey. They travel into the wilderness, far from everyone else, and sit alone to think about life, the universe, and everything. Ma Grakker wept as I set off on my journey, for she knew that my heart was torn—part of it longing for home, part of it longing for the stars—and she feared which way it might go.

"For a long time I wandered through the Friskan swamps, which I love as I love my own feet. But my eyes went always to the stars, until I feared that I was not destined to stay at home and farm worms. For many nights I sat in the sheltering gimbel trees, which would caress me with their furry leaves as I stared at the blazing heavens.

"But much as I loved the stars, I loved the ground beneath my feet even more. By the time the Meditation Journey was over, I knew I wanted to remain at home and continue to be a farmer. This must have showed on my face, for when I returned to the farm, Ma Grakker took one look at me, then threw herself to the floor and began to weep with joy.

"Alas, my difficult decision was made for naught. Unknown to us, and thinking he was doing me a favor, my cousin Rakfratz had put my name in as a candidate for the Galactic Patrol. Two days after I returned from my journey, I received a summons to come to the planetary capital and take the qualifying test."

He paused, and stared at the floor.

"What happened?" I asked at last.

"I achieved the highest grade in the history of Friskalama, over a hundred points above the mark at which service is mandatory. I was drafted, and within the month I found myself on a patrol ship bound for training headquarters." He sighed. "How Ma Grakker wept."

The shadow beneath his brow grew so deep that his eyes seemed to peer out as from a cave.

"Time and coincidence are strange things, Deputy Allbright. In my training class I met both my closest friend and my greatest enemy. The friend, of course, was our dear missing Snout."

He paused for a moment, and a heavy silence fell on the room as we all thought about our lost crew member.

"The enemy," said Grakker when he was ready to continue, "was BKR. Except he was not my enemy at the beginning. In fact for a time I believed him to be my closest friend, while I could barely stand Snout."

"You didn't like Snout?" I asked in surprise.

Grakker actually looked embarrassed. "He had already taken his training as a Mental Master, and I thought he was . . ." He paused, and I could see him groping for the word. "A sissypants," he said at last.

"That is probably not the best word for it," put in Madame Pong, "but it's about the closest your language has to offer, Rod."

Grakker nodded and continued his story. "Of course, at the time no one understood how sadly twisted BKR was, or he would never have been allowed on the patrol. But the little booger had managed to bamboozle the patrol's most sensitive psychometric measures. Alas, something about what we do attracts both the best and the worst of beings. Our job in law enforcement calls to those who want to serve and protect goodness. But it calls, too, to those who long for power for some dark reason of the heart that most of us will never understand.

"I was second in our class. BKR, of course, was at the top. Most of our teachers thought he had a chance to become one of the legends of the Galactic Patrol. I thought so, too.

"Then everything changed. Late one night,

when I could not sleep because I was missing the farm and my dear ma and pa, I went out to look at the stars. I did that sometimes, gazing at my own home star, and imagining the people of Friskalama—the people I had joined the Galactic Patrol in order to protect—going peacefully about their business.

"On this night I saw another figure standing alone in the darkness. When I recognized it as my friend BKR, I decided to creep up on him, to surprise him."

Seeing the look on my face, Grakker said, "I was as mischievous as any other student, Deputy Allbright. But this attempt to scare my friend brought me much deeper fear. For when I was close enough, I could hear what BKR was saying."

Grakker closed his eyes, and I could no longer see beneath his brow at all. "It was a dark moment," he said slowly. "And I would rather it had come to someone else. But it was mine to know. My so-called friend stood with his hands raised to the stars, whispering, 'Every living being is my enemy. When I am done, millions will weep.'

"Then he hugged himself and began to laugh with such evil joy that I felt my blood run cold."

CHAPTER 11

A Worm that Turned

I TRIED TO IMAGINE GRAKKER FRIGHTENED. THE CONcept was too strange for me to wrap my brain around.

"That was pretty weird," I agreed. "But why were you so scared?"

Grakker looked away for a moment. Finally he said, "I believed that BKR was serious. Therefore, I knew I must report what I had heard. But I also knew that I would not be believed."

"Why not?"

"Competition among students was fierce. BKR was not only a beloved student, he was also the only one ahead of me in our class. With him out of the way, *I* would be in first place. So the kind of report I needed to make was likely to be seen as a low and slimy attempt to sabotage a fellow student out of petty personal jealousy."

"What did you do?"

"This matter called more for thought than action. So I swallowed my pride and went to Snout. He understood the seriousness of what I had heard, and in fact had already begun to have doubts of his own about BKR.

"He also understood why it would be pointless to report what I had heard without additional proof.

"That was the beginning of our friendship, though it grew as slowly as a glibbitt blossom on the dark side of Whammus. Together we began to watch BKR. As we did we realized how cleverly he had fooled not only us, but all our teachers. For though he smiled and smiled, his smiles were but a mask to hide his darkness, and when he thought no one was looking, or no one would notice, he committed a thousand tiny cruelties.

"Some were as subtle as making comments that seemed friendly but were carefully phrased to create confusion and self-doubt in the listener. Others were as blatant as tearing the wings from little flying animals, then letting them lose to suffer. But these things he did in private, and we could never catch him at it, only find the sad traces of his cruelty, now that we knew to be looking for it.

"The week before graduation we took everything we had learned to the commander of the academy."

Grakker paused so long that I finally shouted, "So what happened!?"

"They told us we were lying fools and expelled us."

"They threw you out?" I cried in astonishment.

Grakker's answer was interrupted by a shriek from the chibling, which leaped from my shoulder into my lap. I sighed, thinking it was going to cause another fuss.

Before I figured out what had upset it, I heard a gasp from Madame Pong. I turned in the direction she was looking and gasped myself.

Crouching in the entrance to the recreation room was Smorkus Flinders. He held a ray gun in each hand. A smile as wide as the Milky Way split his craggy orange face.

Grakker leaped to his feet. "Put down those guns!" he ordered in his best captain's voice.

I wondered if he thought that would really work. Maybe he just couldn't help himself.

Whatever his reason, it didn't do any good. Smorkus Flinders merely laughed and said, "It's time to trade places, Grakker. I'm going to take over the *Ferkel* for the time being."

"How did you get out?" asked Grakker.

Smorkus Flinders paused. He tipped his head to the side as if he was thinking, then said pleasantly, "You know, I can't come up with a single good reason why I should tell you that." Then his face twisted with rage and he snarled, "Now line up and move out!"

Despite the fact that I was terrified, I waited for orders from Grakker. He hesitated for just a moment, then nodded to us and said, "Line up."

Madame Pong was first, I was second, followed by Tar Gibbons, Phil, and finally Grakker. My fear increased as I walked toward the monster. After all, I was the one who had defeated him while we were in Dimension X. Would he take that out on me now?

I walked past him, half expecting him to lash out at me as I did. What I didn't expect was that the chibling would decide to attack *him*. But as I was passing through the door the purple ball of fur shrieked, launched itself through the air, and wrapped itself around Smorkus Flinders's head.

"Hit the floor!" cried Madame Pong. This was good advice, since the monster immediately began firing both his ray guns. Bolts of energy began zinging across the room.

That didn't stop our Master of the Martial Arts. "Hee-yah! Frizzim Spezzack!" cried Tar Gibbons as it launched itself at the monster.

The chibling was shrieking. Smorkus Flinders was roaring in anger. The Tar was dodging energy rays, moving so fast its arms and legs were almost a blur.

Smorkus Flinders dropped one of his ray guns and began to claw at the chibling, trying to tear it from his face.

I wondered if I should go after the gun. But the monster continued his blind firing of the other gun, and those random shots were too terrifying for me. So I stayed huddled behind a chair. I am not proud of that, but I am not particularly ashamed, either. Warrior Science teaches us to save the valiant gesture for the moment when being a fool is the wisest thing to do.

I could not do what the Tar was doing, and it would gain nothing for me to be sliced to ribbons.

As it turned out, the Tar couldn't do it for long, either. Less than a minute later a stray ray of light sizzled through its shoulder. My teacher made no cry of pain, simply fell twitching to the floor.

I watched, frozen in horror. I was terrified that the random firing of the ray gun might connect again and kill the Tar—and equally terrified that if I tried to drag my teacher to safety, I might not last more than a few seconds myself.

In that instant Smorkus Flinders finally managed to rip the chibling from his face. Roaring with pain and rage, he flung it across the room.

"Eee-e-e-eep!" it cried as it flew. Then the brave little creature hit the wall with a sickening smack and fell silent. It slid to the floor, where it lay still and unmoving.

I cried out. Was it dead?

If so, it had died for nothing, since Smorkus Flinders was still in charge. Pointing his ray gun at the fallen Tar, he bellowed, "Don't anyone move! Don't even twitch, or I toast the bugman!"

None of us twitched.

"Madame Pong, get in here where I can see you."

With quiet dignity Madame Pong walked back into the room.

Again the monster told us to line up. The Tar, badly wounded, was unable to stand by itself. I was relieved when Smorkus Flinders ordered me to help my teacher to its feet. As the Tar's krev-lik, it was my proper job.

This time the monster was taking no chances. At his direction Madame Pong bound Grakker's hands. Then she used a length of cord to bind me to the Tar, so that neither of us could move freely, but I could still hold it up. Smorkus Flinders hesitated for a while over what to do with Phil. Finally he had Madame Pong wrap about a hundred feet of cord around the plant so that he couldn't even wave his leaves.

I think poor Plink was trapped inside.

When Madame Pong was the only one left, Smorkus Flinders bound her hands behind her back as well, then marched us out of the recreation room.

As we left, I glanced over my shoulder at the chibling. It had not moved from where it fell. But I heard it make a tiny "Eeeep!"

The sound tore at my heart.

Smorkus Flinders herded us into the conference room then wrapped the rest of us in as much cord as he had put around Phil.

I had seen so many movies where people managed to get out of being tied up that when Smorkus Flinders left the room, I thought maybe this would all turn out to be a minor problem. I was *sure* one of us would be able to wriggle free somehow.

Even if that had been true—and I soon began to suspect it wasn't—a while later Smorkus Flinders returned with a sack of the blue rings we had used to keep him in place while we interrogated him. He smiled as he put them around our necks.

"I would prefer to simply toss you into space," he said. "Or fry you, or grind you up or something. But my partner might not like that. He may have some better use for you."

I had to hold my breath while he was speaking. His own breath smelled as if something had crawled into his lungs, died, and begun to rot.

When he left the room again, I whispered, "Is there any way out of these?"

"None that I know of," replied Grakker, his voice heavy with despair. "Forgive me, my crew. It appears we have disgraced ourselves for nothing."

"Look at it this way, Captain," burped Phil. "Given what Smorkus Flinders is likely to do to us, we won't need to worry about what Galactic Headquarters thinks!"

His voice was muffled by the layers of cord surrounding him.

I hated the way the blue rings felt. Well, that's not quite accurate. I couldn't *feel* them at all. I just couldn't move anything from my neck down, not even wiggle my toes. It was frustrating—and terrifying in a way. A bubble of anxiety began slowly swelling in my chest. I wanted to scream, but managed to hold it in.

Time dragged on. I wished I could turn off my brain, so I could stop worrying about my father, about Snout, about my mother and the twins, about BKR and whatever his horrible plan was, about the poor chibling lying wounded in the rec room.

Hunger began to gnaw at my belly.

I tried counting Phil's petals, but gave up because I knew I could never see all of them.

I don't know how much time had gone by when Tar Gibbons whispered, "Someone's coming!"

I started to ask it how it knew, but it hissed me to silence. A moment later I heard the sound too.

Footsteps, but too light to be those of Smorkus Flinders.

But if not him, then who?

CHAPTER 12

Split Personality

I WAS STILL TRYING TO FIGURE OUT WHO IT COULD BE when a familiar voice called, "Rod? Rod, where the heck are you?"

Elspeth!

My heart rose and sank in a single instant. She was our one hope for getting out of this mess. But if she didn't shut up, Smorkus Flinders would catch her before she could do us any good.

I listened with dread, expecting to hear the sound of Smorkus Flinders capturing her at any moment. I wanted to cry out a warning, but feared it would only increase the chances of the monster realizing she was on the loose.

Elspeth continued walking toward us. When she was only a few feet from our door, I hissed, "Elspeth! In here!"

She grinned when she walked into the room.

"There you are! I've been looking everywhere for you guys!"

"Shhhh!" I hissed desperately. "Smorkus Flinders is on the loose. You don't want him to hear you!"

She laughed. "Oh, don't worry about that turkey!"

"What do you mean?" asked Grakker.

Elspeth waved her hands as if the monster was a minor detail. "I put him in suspended animation about twenty minutes ago."

We stared at her in astonishment.

Elspeth smiled. "I bet you'd like me to let you loose, wouldn't you?"

"Like it?" roared Grakker. "I *order* you to free us instantly."

"You could order me if I was a member of the Galactic Patrol," said Elspeth. "But you told me I couldn't join. So you don't get to give me orders."

I thought Grakker's eyes were going to bulge right out of his head. "Undo these rings this instant!"

"They're probably too complicated for me," said Elspeth, settling to the floor. "After all, I'm just a little girl. I suppose I might be able to work it out. But I think we should talk first. I might want to cut a deal here."

The rumble in Grakker's throat was something

like the sound I imagine an angry tiger must make.

"Captain, let me," said Madame Pong. I could tell she was dying to get up and switch modules on him. She probably wished Elspeth had a head where you could switch modules, too.

Grakker grumbled, but nodded.

"Elspeth, I know you're angry," said Madame Pong.

"Angry!" shouted Elspeth, scrambling to her feet. "Just because you're such snots you would put a little kid in suspended animation? Why would that make me *angry?"*

"Why don't you tell us how you dealt with Smorkus Flinders?" said Madame Pong soothingly.

Elspeth smiled, and I realized again how clever Madame Pong was.

"Well," said Elspeth, "when I woke up and there was no one waiting to greet me, I wondered where everyone was. I mean, even though you're the kind of creeps who would freeze a kid just because she wanted to come on an adventure, I figured unless something had gone really wrong, at least Madame Pong would be there. I thought maybe you had all died in some horrible accident and I had been drifting for five thousand years in suspended animation and was lost in the deepest part of space and had only woken up because some horrible creature had gotten on board and disturbed the ship's systems or something.

"So I got out of my pod very quietly, just in case."

I happened to know from personal experience that Elspeth can be *very* quiet when she wants to be, since she had snuck up on me dozens of times over the last few years. I was glad she had finally found a good use for her talent.

"It was pretty scary when I couldn't find any of you," she continued. "I was about to start yelling for help, just to see if anyone would come, when I heard Smorkus Flinders crashing around on the bridge.

"Actually, I didn't know it was Smorkus Flinders. I just knew I heard someone. So I snuck up and peeked through the door. When I saw who it was, I scooted away and went looking for a ray gun. I finally found one in Grakker's room. After that it was easy to take the monster by surprise. I suppose he figured everyone on the ship was already here in this room, since it would probably never occur to him that you would actually freeze a kid.

"I would have settled things faster, but I don't think he believed I would really use the gun."

"Why not?" asked Madame Pong.

"Because he said, 'Put the gun down, little girl. You might hurt yourself.' "

I almost felt sorry for Smorkus Flinders. He couldn't have known what a dumb thing that was to say to Elspeth.

"How did you convince him that you *would* use it?" asked Madame Pong.

Elspeth shrugged. "I zapped him a couple of times. Then he believed me. I made him get into one of those pods and froze him. Then I came looking for you guys."

"That was very well done," said Madame Pong.

Elspeth scowled. "Do you really think so? Or are you just saying that so I'll let you go?"

"*I* think it was well done," I said.

Elspeth smiled. "I know *he* means it. Roddie never lies. Well, hardly ever. I guess you guys have been teaching him." She sighed. "All right, I'll let you go *if* you promise not to freeze me again, and to let me join the Galactic Patrol."

Madame Pong shook her head. "I can promise the first, but not the second."

"Why not?" demanded Elspeth, stamping her foot. "Because I'm a girl?"

I considered pointing out that this was a pretty stupid question to ask of a female crew member, but decided to keep my mouth shut.

"No," said Madame Pong slowly. "Because you're not a citizen of the galaxy."

Elspeth looked startled. But she had heard Madame Pong say the same thing to my mother, so she knew it was true.

"I'm sorry," said Madame Pong. "This is not something I can change. I do not run the galaxy."

Elspeth sighed. "If I let you out, will you promise to try to get that stupid rule changed?"

Madame Pong smiled. *"When* you let us out, I promise to tell you why no one in the galactic government will listen to a word any of us says right now, which I think you will find fairly interesting. And, with the captain's permission, I promise that we will not freeze you again."

She glanced at Grakker for confirmation. When he grunted his assent, Elspeth said, "Okay, how do I undo these ring thingies?"

As soon as Elspeth got me loose, I turned to Grakker and said, "Request permission to go check on the chibling, sir."

He nodded, and I raced out of the room.

The recreation room was a disaster from the battle with Smorkus Flinders. Despite the debris, it didn't take me more than a few seconds to spot the chibling. It was still lying exactly where it had fallen.

My heart sank. It had been hours since it had fallen here. If it hadn't moved, it was almost certainly dead.

Sadly I reached down to pick up its little body.

I drew my hand back in shock. The chibling was still warm!

Was it possible it wasn't dead after all?

Gently I tucked my hands around its body.

When I lifted it up, it broke in half!

I think I must have screamed. In any event the others came rushing in to see what was wrong—even Tar Gibbons, though it was moving much more slowly than the rest.

"Look!" I cried, holding out the two halves of the chibling. "Look what happened!"

Madame Pong took the pieces of chibling from me and stared at them in puzzlement. "Both parts feel as if they are alive," she said at last. "We had better put them on a healing table."

Gulping hard, trying not to cry, I agreed. I hadn't realized I had become so attached to the little critter.

With Phil's help, I tucked the two parts of the chibling together on one of the healing tables while Madame Pong and Grakker helped Tar Gibbons onto the table next to it.

The blue lights came on, bathing both our wounded warriors in healing rays.

"Permission to remain in sick bay, Captain?" I asked.

Grakker hesitated, then nodded.

The others left for a meeting.

I sat between Tar Gibbons and the broken chibling for some time. When it finally became clear that nothing was going to happen to the chibling right away, the Tar said, "I will watch over the creature for you, my krevlik. You had best report to duty."

Reluctantly I left the room.

I found the others in the conference room.

"What I want to know," burped Phil as I entered and took my place, "is how Smorkus Flinders got loose to begin with. I checked the Sus-An Pod myself just before we put him in it. I'm sure it was working all right."

"Perhaps some minor difference in the metabolism of a being from Dimension X rendered the pod ineffective," suggested Madame Pong.

"That would make sense," said Grakker. "But it means we'll have to mount a round-the-clock watch on his pod so he doesn't escape again. Deputy Allbright, I want you to take the first shift. Normally I would ask the Tar, but it will have to spend some time in sick bay before it can do this kind of service. As its krevlik, it is reasonable for you to assume this duty."

I sighed and went down to the Sus-An Room. Fortunately, I was able to stop at my room along the way. I picked up my book and spent the next few hours studying the method by which the *Ferkel* hopped between dimensions.

When Phil came to take my place, I went to the recreation room to get something to eat. Elspeth was trying to do the same thing, without much success.

"This food stinks!" she said as I came through the door.

"You don't have to eat it," Madame Pong replied gently.

Elspeth snorted. "Great. I save your butts, and now you're going to starve me."

Things had definitely been quieter around here while she was in suspended animation.

I joined her at the table. I had to admit that Elspeth was right about the food. I still hadn't been able to get the synthesizer to make stuff taste the way it did at home. But I had found a few alien things that I liked, especially a dish called scrambled squibbish. I dialed up a couple of servings of it, one for each of us.

"What's *that?*" Elspeth asked in horror when I set the plates on the table.

"Try it. It's better than it looks."

"That wouldn't be hard," she muttered, which was true, since the stuff looked like moldy rat tails sauteed in eyeball sauce. "You go first."

After she saw me take a bite and not gag, she

closed her eyes and took a bite herself. "Not bad," she said. "Tastes sort of like chicken."

I went to bed early that night, both because I was exhausted, and because we were scheduled to arrive at the Mentat the next day.

Before I turned in I went to give my respects to the Tar, who was almost totally healed, and to check on the chibling.

When I saw it, I cried out in horror.

"What's happening?"

"I do not know, my krevlik," replied the Tar. "This transformation began just a short time ago."

One part of the chibling was just as it had always been: purple, fuzzy, and warm. But the other part had lost all its fur. I would have worried that it was dead, except it had also gotten larger—almost twice as big as it had been.

I reached out to touch it, then drew my hand back and shivered. The blue skin was smooth and slick, and I could feel a pulse running underneath it.

For two hours I sat between the Tar and the broken chibling, watching fearfully to see what it might do.

Nothing happened.

Finally the Tar said, "I think you should sleep, my krevlik. I will keep an eye on it."

Since I had been nodding in my chair anyway, I finally agreed.

Yet once I was back in my room, sleep did not come easily. In addition to my worry about the chibling, I was excited because we were expecting to arrive at the Mentat the next day. Assuming that the Galactic Patrol wasn't waiting there to arrest us, we should find the answer to at least one of our mysteries when we got there.

I don't know how long went by before I finally drifted off. Nor do I know how much longer it was before I was woken by a feeling of pressure on my chest.

I opened my eyes, then cried out in horrified surprise.

Staring back at me was a single, enormous eyeball.

Before I could make another sound, it sent a message into my head.

Hi, Uncle Rod. Want to get up and play?

CHAPTER 13

Seymour

AT HOME I WOULD HAVE SCREAMED AND FLUNG ASIDE the covers. My mother would have been at my side in a moment.

But I had no covers, and since I was floating in my antigravity bed, I had nothing to push against to do any flinging anyway. I did scream, but my room was soundproof, so the only effect it had was to upset the eyeball. I could actually feel it flinching.

What did you do that for? it thought.

It sounded so genuinely puzzled—and so basically friendly—that I held in my next scream and tried to get my racing heart under control. Using a breathing technique Tar Gibbons had taught me, I was soon calm again.

In the moments it took me to settle myself, my eyes began to adjust to the dark. Combined with the fact that the room had sensed my waking movements and automatically begun to raise the light level, I as soon able to get a good look at the creature crouched on my chest.

It turned out not to be merely an eyeball—though the eyeball was certainly its most prominent feature. In fact, its head consisted of nothing but a single eyeball the size of my fist. No nose, no mouth, no ears: just that huge eye, which was sheathed in blue skin, and located at the end of a snaky blue neck that led to a four-legged body about the size and shape of a large cat. (Well, a sort of squashed, ridged, naked blue cat. But you get the idea.) Each of its four feet had two blobby, clawless toes. It had a thick tail, which looked a lot like its neck, only minus the eyeball.

Since the thing had spoken in my head—a sensation I was getting used to by this time—I thought a message back to it: *Who are you?*

I'm your chibling, silly. Not your silly chibling—that's the other part of me.

My shock and disbelief must have been so intense that they were painful. At least, the creature recoiled a little, blinking. (And when this thing blinked, you really noticed it.)

I see you don't believe me.

Well, it does seem unlikely, I replied, wishing the thing would just go away. Nervously I wondered if it could pick up that wish from my mind.

If it did pick up the nasty thought, it chose to

ignore it and just sent, *The rest of me is still the same idiotic ball of fur it's always been, if that makes you feel any better.*

Where is it?

Still healing, replied the creature. *That half was in worse shape than I was after yesterday's fight. That's why I'm here now, by the way. I'm a little early. But the trauma of being flung against the wall threw us into transformation stage ahead of schedule.*

Now that I was fairly certain the creature wasn't going to attack me, I felt myself relax a little. *Could you explain things more clearly?* I asked.

Sure! Here's the deal. We chiblings have several life stages. Stage two is the fuzzy-ball stage, when we have to attach ourself to someone—to some sentient being. Once we're attached, we tap our host's brain, which is how we learn. That's why I think in your language, by the way. It's my birth language, of sorts.

Do you have a name? I asked.

Did you give me one? it replied sharply. *Hah! Double hah! I have to tell you, Uncle Rod, it really hurt my feelings that you never bothered to name me.*

I could feel myself blushing in the half-darkness. *In case you hadn't noticed, there's been a lot going on,* I thought defensively. *And*

I never quite got used to having you hang on to me like that all the time. It's not like I asked *you to attach yourself to me.*

The thought felt cruel, and I immediately wished I could take it back. On the other hand, it was also true. Sometimes I had a hard time figuring out which was worse: lying or being cruel.

Do you think I would have picked you if I had a choice? replied the chibling.

Now I was the one who was offended! *What do you mean by that?*

It's a biological imperative. When a chibling enters second stage, it has to bond with the first sentient creature it can make mental contact with. You were it. Given a chance, I would have been glad to pick someone older, wiser, and more compassionate. As it is, I got you.

Geez, this thing really knew how to hurt a guy.

I'm working on all that, I responded.

I'm sure you'll have no problem with at least one of them, it replied. *I've noticed you're getting older by the minute.*

Great. I was mentally attached to the world's most sarcastic fluff ball. Or the brain that went with the fluff ball. Or something.

Let's work on the name thing, I thought, mostly to change the subject. *How about Chip?*

The chibling made gagging noises in my head.

Chip the Chibling? Oh, please! Why not just name me 'Fluffy Cutesy-buttons' and get it over with? Yetch. Yetch yetch yetch!

Do you have a better suggestion? I thought testily.

How about Seymour?

Seymour?

Yeah, it's a joke. Get it? Yoo-hoo! Rod, this is your wake-up call. Take a look at me. I'm like, all eyeball. So I'm Seymour. See More. Get it? Get it?

And you thought Chip was bad?

At least this has a little flair, replied the chibling. *And you have to remember, I'm still fairly new at this. I thought it was pretty good.*

So Seymour it was.

The other half of the chibling showed up sometime during the night, seemingly completely healed.

We're all together again! thought Seymour happily.

So what do we call this half of you? I asked. *Seymour, Part One?*

Too confusing, replied Seymour. *How about Edgar?*

Is that supposed to be some sort of a joke? I asked suspiciously.

No, I just like the name.

Since the fuzzball was really part of Seymour, I figured he should have the right to choose. So Edgar it was.

I came to breakfast the next morning with Edgar clinging to my shoulder and Seymour walking beside me like a one-eyed bald blue cat. The rest of the crew was appropriately astonished.

"Where did *that* come from?" roared Grakker, pointing to Seymour.

"It's stage three of the chibling," I replied. "The intelligent part. Or so it claims."

No need to be snippy, Seymour said in my head.

"What do you mean, so it claims?" asked Tar Gibbons. "Does it talk to you?"

"It talks directly into my head. I'm starting to get used to it."

"Where's its mouth?" asked Elspeth. She was squatting in front of Seymour, staring him in the eye. Given how much she uses her own mouth, it figured that that would be the first thing she'd wonder about.

"In its other part," I said, gesturing to the furry lump on my shoulder.

"Now that sounds interesting," said Phil. "From a purely technical standpoint, if nothing else. Care to explain, Deputy Allbright?"

Stop me if I get any of this wrong, I thought to Seymour.

Out loud, I said, "Well, it turns out that a mature chibling is a two-part animal. The little fluffy part—his name is Edgar, by the way—does the eating. And Seymour here does the thinking."

"Now there's a genuine brain-body dichotomy for you," said Tar Gibbons, tucking a still-squirming leg from its breakfast back between its lips.

"If that part does the thinking, then where does it keep its brain?" asked Elspeth. "The head looks like it's nothing but one big eyeball."

"It is," I replied. "The brain is down here." I pointed to what you would expect to be Seymour's stomach. "That's *all* brain. And from what he tells me, he's got some growing to do. He claims his brain is going to be very big."

Elspeth looked as confused as I had felt the night before. "If it has no mouth, and its stomach is really its brain, what does it do about eating?"

"The other part does the eating, and sends energy to Seymour via some kind of microwave or something. I think he picks up the rays through that huge eye."

"Whoa!" said Elspeth admiringly. "That is extremely weird."

You ain't seen nothin' yet, thought Seymour.

* * *

By the time we reached Planet Mentat that afternoon, I was used to having Seymour around and communicating with me. We were working the control room with Phil when we popped out of the last alternate dimension and back into Dimension Q.

Phil had the viewscreen on, and we could see the Mentat's planet floating in space ahead of us. It had three brilliant rings—two wide green ones, separated by a narrow orange one—and at least twenty small moons. It was one of the most wonderful things I had ever seen. We called Elspeth so that she could come see it, too.

I was surprised to realize that for all my adventures with the aliens, this would be the first alien planet that I had visited, or at least the first in my own dimension.

As we approached, Grakker and Madame Pong spent a lot of time on the radio getting clearances.

We dropped even closer to the surface.

"There," said Madame Pong, who had joined us. "That's the Mentat—the school where all Mental Masters are trained."

"That?" I asked in astonishment.

CHAPTER 14

Into the Mentat

"IT'S SO BIG!" SAID ELSPETH, HER VOICE FILLED WITH awe.

"I don't care how big it is," I said. "It's a *plant!*"

Brilliant, said Seymour. *I feel privileged to share your brain.*

How to describe the Mentat?

I'll start with Phil's words: "As far as we know, it is the largest living thing in the galaxy," he burped proudly. "It is an object of great veneration for my family. In fact, I have an uncle who claims our family tree is related to it. But I am not certain that is true."

To be more specific . . .

Imagine an area about two football fields long and three football fields wide. That's to give you the ground space.

Now round off the corners.

Now imagine a tree stump big enough to *cover* all that space. Not a full tree; that would be *miles* high. Just the stump, which would still be several hundred feet high.

Now you've got the size, shape, and the general look.

The roof of the stump appears to be made of red seaweed. Its outer walls are covered with thick brown bark, just as a tree would be. But in those walls are hundreds, maybe thousands of windows. They have no glass, but they do have covers that can be closed over them like shutters. The covers aren't nailed on. They're part of the plant, grown that way.

The top of the Mentat is a rolling area from which dozens of towers stretch up like saplings. Some of the bigger ones, as much as forty or fifty feet across, rise thousands of feet above the stump. Tubular structures stretch between some of the towers. I learned later that they were hollow—sort of like covered bridges. Thick, moss-like substances—rusty-red, green, and brown—drape from them in graceful, trailing arcs.

Thousands of robed beings moved in and out of the building, most walking in a slow, stately way—though here and there you could see someone zipping their way between them.

"This is the coolest place I ever saw," said Elspeth.

Me, too, thought Seymour. *But then, it's just about the first place I've ever seen.*

We enlarged the ship and landed in a field about a half mile from the Mentat. When Elspeth and I left the ship, Tar Gibbons gave us an extra shot of the enlarging ray, to increase us to our full size.

The Tar stayed on board for two reasons: 1) to guard Smorkus Flinders so he couldn't escape again and (2) so that Phil, who would normally have been the one to stay aboard, could make a pilgrimage to the giant plant.

A group of beings came walking across the field to greet us. They were about the same height as the crew of the *Ferkel,* which is to say they stood slightly higher than my waist.

The leader of the group was slender and tight looking. She had gray skin and large, multifaceted eyes that made me think of the close-up photographs I had seen of flies. Two beings stood right behind her. One looked like a small green haystack. The other had a scaly scarlet face that made him look something like the goldfish I won for Little Thing Two at the county fair. A few paces back stood five or six more, all of them equally strange looking.

The leader said something, but since she was not using an English language module as the crew did, I couldn't understand a word of it. This was the first time in our travels that I had run into this problem, and I found it very frustrating.

Madame Pong removed her own language module and replied in what I later learned was Standard Galactic.

Reinserting the module behind her ear, she turned to Elspeth and me and said, "The gray one's name is Arly Bung. She is chief of security for the Mentat. She offers us cautious welcome, and hospitality for the night."

"It doesn't sound like they're thrilled to see us," I said.

"They're not. They don't think much of the Galactic Patrol. Of course, the Galactic Patrol itself doesn't think much of *us* at the moment. It will be interesting to see how we are greeted by the Heads of the Mentat. If they know we have gone renegade, they might turn us in—or they might not care at all."

As we walked to the huge living building, I had a strange sense that someone was watching us. But try as I might, I couldn't spot anyone.

The road to the Mentat was filled by the widest assortment of creatures you could imagine. I saw beings covered with flesh, feathers, and scales, but many more wrapped in bodies unlike anything I had ever imagined: smooth, lumpy, spiky, slimy—you name it, it was here.

Given this incredible diversity, you would have thought nothing would stand out as unusual enough to attract attention. But two things did—and it wasn't Seymour and Edgar. It was me and Elspeth.

What made us stand out was our height; we towered above the rest of the creatures. So many of them looked up at us and made noises that I took to be dismay that I truly wished we had stayed at half size.

The road led to a door so wide ten beings could walk through it at once. Engraved in the wood above it were the words NO MATTER HOW DEEP YOU GO, THERE'S ALWAYS ANOTHER LEVEL.

I couldn't read it myself, of course, since it was carved in Standard Galactic. Madame Pong translated it for me and Elspeth.

"It's the Mentat's motto," she added.

The door led into a chamber twice the size of my school gymnasium. Light streamed in through windows in the upper sections. Wide wooden paths sloped up along the walls.

Instead of taking those paths, Arly Bung led us to an opening in the far wall. Dismissing all but two of her guards, she ushered us into a moss-lined bubble the size of Mom's Chevrolet. A panel slid shut behind us, and the bubble began to move. I wondered if it was powered mechanically, or if we had actually stepped into the plant's circulation system.

The bubble was like an elevator, except that it not only went up, it went from side to side. When it finally stopped, it had carried us high into one of the towers.

Arly Bung said something.

"These will be our rooms," translated Madame Pong.

"Neat!" said Elspeth.

I felt the same way. The room we were facing was wonderfully warm and cozy. It looked as if everything—sitting surfaces, tables, resting areas—had been carved from a single huge block of wood.

When I said this, Madame Pong translated it for our hosts.

"Thank you," replied Arly Bung, via Madame Pong. Looking up at me, she wrinkled her gray face and added, "If we had had more notice that you were coming—and were so *big*—we would have grown something more suitable to your size."

That was when I realized I had been wrong. Nothing in the room was carved. The whole thing had simply *grown* that way.

Arly Bung said a few more things to Madame Pong. Then she and the guards left, closing the door behind them.

"Are we prisoners?" I asked.

"Only of our own courtesy," replied Madame Pong. "We can come and go as we please. However, they would rather we didn't, since we make them nervous. So we won't, unless it is necessary. They said we will be able to meet with the Head Council this evening."

"What is this place, anyway?" asked Elspeth, poking at a mossy-looking cushion. She decided it was soft enough and plunked herself down on it.

"It is the single most important spot in the galaxy for those who wish to pursue a life of the mind," replied Madame Pong.

Maybe we should move here, Uncle Rod, sent Seymour. *It would probably be good for both of us.*

"I'm confused," I said, ignoring the chibling. "I thought the Mentat was a place where beings like Snout came to be trained as Mental Masters so they could be part of the Galactic Patrol."

Grakker snorted. "The Mentat provides the patrol with a few Mental Masters every year, in return for the patrol's protection. But they don't like the idea much. From what Snout told me, they look down on the beings who agree to do it." He snorted again. "If you ask me, they're a bunch of snooty boogers."

* * *

An hour or so after we had settled in the room, someone came to talk to Grakker and Madame Pong. I couldn't understand a word they said, because they took out their language implants and spoke in Standard Galactic.

After they were gone, Madame Pong came to Elspeth and me and said, "The Mentat has generously offered to install language implants in your brains so that you can speak Standard Galactic."

"They want to do brain surgery on me?" I asked nervously.

Don't let them amputate me, Uncle Rod! wailed Seymour, his distress so strong it made me wince.

"Don't they have to shave off all your hair for that?" asked Elspeth, putting her hand to her head.

Madame Pong smiled. "On *your* planet, certainly. But here, it is a minor operation. You'll be in and out in fifteen minutes."

What about me? thought Seymour. *I don't want to end up the only being in the whole crew who can't understand Standard Galactic!*

I thought you could understand whatever I thought, I thought.

Not if you start thinking in another language! he replied, panic making his thoughts sharp as vinegar.

So Seymour had the operation, too, and when

Arly Bung came to summon the crew to meet the Head Council three hours later, Elspeth, Seymour, and I all went as fluent speakers (or thinkers, in Seymour's case) of Standard Galactic.

I could barely feel the lump behind my ear where they had installed the language implant. But it was weird to open my mouth and have sounds I had never made before come floating out—and even weirder that I could understand them.

"Holy mackerel," whispered Elspeth when we walked into the council chamber. "They weren't kidding, calling this the Head Council!"

I was trying too hard not to barf to answer her.

CHAPTER 15

The Head Council

IF I HAD BEEN ABLE TO TALK, I WOULD HAVE JOKED that they ought to have called the group the Head*less* Council. Bodiless, too, since the council consisted of a circle of thirteen *brains* of all sizes, shapes, and colors. Each brain rested in a clear, liquid-filled tank. Thick vines connected the tanks. Mounted on the front of each tank was a small box through which the brains spoke.

"Greetings," said a large brown brain. "How may we help you?"

I had expected the voice to sound mechanical, but it was warm and soft as any living being's. I kept forgetting that just because a piece of equipment resembled something we use on Earth, I couldn't expect it to have the same limitations.

"Greetings," replied Madame Pong. "And thank you for receiving us." She made a little bow. I wondered if she thought the heads could see her somehow, or if she just did it out of habit.

"To receive you is neither our pleasure nor our privilege," replied another brain. "It is, however, our duty, since we use the services of the Galactic Patrol. We make the assumption that you have followed our agreement with the patrol, and only come here because it is necessary."

These guys were even more painfully honest than I was!

Madame Pong put her hands together, palm to palm, in front of her. "We come at the request of one of your own—the Mental Master Flinge Iblik, who was once part of our crew." I noticed she managed to avoid speaking about the Galactic Patrol at all.

(I also noticed that she used Snout's formal name, and wondered what the Head Council would think of his nickname.)

"Flinge Iblik was not only our ship's Mental Master, but our esteemed companion," continued Madame Pong. "He vanished mysteriously while we were on a mission in Dimension X. However, since that time he has contacted Deputy Allbright here on three occasions. On two of those occasions Flinge Iblik told Deputy Allbright that he was being held by something called 'the Ferkada.' "

You could feel the change in the room when

Madame Pong mentioned the Ferkada. It was as if she had just done something rude, or dangerous.

"I have done an extensive search," she continued. "But in all our diplomatic and historic files, I could find only the most fleeting mention of this name—never anything more substantial than 'it was also rumored that something called the Ferkada was involved in this situation.' "

Bowing apologetically, she said, "It is not our wish to disturb you. But Flinge Iblik asked us to come to you for help. And so here we are."

"We need to speak to Deputy Allbright," said the smallest of the red brains.

"Here, sir," I replied nervously. Immediately I felt stupid. Who knew whether the brain I was speaking to had been male or female back when it was still in its body? For that matter, maybe it was like the Tar, and had been something else altogether.

"Are you willing to submit to a mind probe?" asked the brains, speaking in unison this time. The sound was soft and pleasant. Even so, I found it a little scary.

It's okay with me, thought Seymour. *I don't have any nasty secrets. I haven't been around long enough.*

I glanced at Madame Pong. She gestured to Grakker, who looked annoyed that I hadn't checked with him first. But I couldn't keep track of which one of them was in charge when we were out of the ship.

What I did know—because I had already been through this once when we were in Dimension X—was that Provision 136.9.17.48 of the Galactic Code forbade them to *force* anyone to undergo a mind probe. The question had come up partly because the last probe I had been asked to submit to had been somewhat dangerous. I figured this one would be a lot safer. After all, these brains were clearly *the* galactic experts when it came to this kind of thing. I was checking with Grakker and Madame Pong not because I was frightened, but simply to see whether they thought it was a good idea.

Grakker nodded.

"Probe away," I said, trying to sound braver than I felt.

"Please step into the center of the circle."

I peeled the furry part of the chibling off my shoulder and handed it to Elspeth. As I stepped forward, Seymour whispered in my brain, *Good luck, Uncle Rod.*

The probe started immediately. The last time I had experienced this kind of thing was with the Ting Wongovia. But while he was learning about me, I had also learned about him. This time I felt and saw nothing.

I'm not sure, but I think the whole thing only

took a few seconds. When the brains were done, they said, "In regard to the Ferkada, we cannot be of any help. However, there is one thing we can do for you that may be of some help."

"What?" growled Grakker. I could tell he was bitterly disappointed that the Head Council had given us so little information. I was, too, for that matter. Why had Snout sent us here?

Had the messages been fake after all? My stomach churned.

"We are willing to take the monster Smorkus Flinders off your hands. We may be able to reverse the damage done to him by the reality quakes in Dimension X—although that will be a long and difficult process."

Madame Pong glanced at Grakker, then nodded. "That would be deeply appreciated."

Naturally *I* was sent to the ship to help Tar Gibbons bring Smorkus Flinders into the Mentat. (I was beginning to realize that being a deputy meant a lot of running and fetching.)

Arly Bung and two of her assistants came along as well, which made me sort of irritated, since I felt like they didn't trust me.

When we brought Smorkus Flinders out from the ship, we enlarged him only to standard alien size. So now instead of being twice as tall as me (four inches to my two inches), he only stood slightly higher than my waist. If the Tar had not been standing right beside me, I might have forgotten how often I had been told that a warrior should be gracious in victory.

As we returned to the Mentat, I again had that strange sense that someone was watching us as we traveled. But no matter how fast I spun around, I couldn't spot anyone.

I expressed my concerns to Seymour, and asked him to keep an eye out.

I don't have much choice, he replied.

The robed students gave us a wide berth as we entered the Mentat. I couldn't blame them. Even in captivity, Smorkus Flinders was pretty frightening.

Some of the students began to chant as we passed. I had a feeling they were doing the mental version of spraying an air freshener.

As soon as the Tar and I (and the chiblings, part one and part two) brought the monster to the Head Council, the brains began to question him. They asked him three or four simple things to start off, all of which he answered in a very straightforward way.

Then they asked, "When did you first meet BKR?"

"That I cannot tell you," he said, without a trace of emotion in his voice.

A murmur of surprise rippled around the ring of brains.

"Why not?" asked the one shaped like a loaf of French bread, its electronic voice surprisingly sharp.

His face as still as if he was in a trance, Smorkus Flinders said, "I have a block in my brain that prevents me from responding."

"Who put that block there?"

His face suddenly coming to life again, Smorkus Flinders roared, *"I did, you morons!"*

Though the words came from the mouth of the monster, it was pretty clear he was no longer speaking for himself, that someone else was speaking through him.

"Just who are we addressing now?" asked the brains calmly.

"Me? Let's just say that I'm the kind of guy who likes to see people in misery. Some people call me BKR. Grakker used to think I was a friend. Rod used to think I was an enemy. Hey, Rod, I saw your dad the other day. He looks *horrible.* He said to tell you hello. Well, I think that was what he said. He was having a hard time getting his words out, what with that collar around his neck."

CHAPTER 16

Roots

MY ENTIRE BODY WENT TIGHT. I WANTED TO LAUNCH myself at Smorkus Flinders and pound him to a pulp. But that would have been pointless, since it wasn't actually him talking.

Madame Pong put her hand on my shoulder and whispered, "Remember, Rod—if you believe him, he wins."

I nodded. BKR was a tremendous liar who would gladly say anything he thought might cause someone pain.

The problem is, even liars tell the truth sometimes.

"What do you want, BKR?" growled Grakker.

The laugh that came from Smorkus Flinders's mouth was short, harsh, ugly. "Me? Why, I'm a simple boy, Grakker old chum. I could easily be satisfied by, say, a *galaxy-wide tragedy.*" He laughed again. "Ah, I can just see you moving into hero mode. Or maybe Madame Pong is sticking some hero module into your head. Hey, MP—how ya doing, babe? If you get sick of that stiff Grakker, send me a message and you can give a real man a try."

Madame Pong's face showed no emotions at all. If BKR's insolence was getting to her, she hid it well.

"Tell you what, kids," said BKR. "I'll give you a chance to stop me. Just meet me at the end of time, and we'll thrash this out. We can have a party. I'll be there. Rod's dad will be there. Maybe Snout will even be there. You guys bring the snacks—maybe some of those little flying things Tar Gibbons likes to munch on. Until then, this is WBKR in wouldn't-you-like-to-know-where, signing off. This program sponsored by End of Life As We Know It Productions. Remember, we're closer than you think."

Smorkus Flinders's face, which had been lively and animated as BKR spoke through him, suddenly went blank.

"What a distasteful creature," said the big blue brain.

"Absolutely," agreed one of the lavender ones. "But the main question is: How much truth was there in what he said?"

"Based on a voice analysis, as well as the nature of the brain activity stimulated within

Smorkus Flinders's head, I would say it was about half true," said the smallest of the red brains.

"Which parts?" I cried out, unable to restrain myself any longer. "Which parts were true?"

"Ah," said the brain sadly. "If only we knew. . . ."

"How does he do that?" demanded Grakker.

"Pretty much the same way that Snout communicates with young Rod Allbright here. Did we explain that, by the way? It's quite unusual."

"No, you didn't explain," I said sharply. "How *does* he do it?"

"Well, there are tiny traces of his brain lodged inside yours—"

"What?" I cried, grabbing my head.

"It happened when you prematurely severed the training transfer Flinge Iblik had set up to teach you how to use your flying belt," said the square green brain.

"How do you know about that?"

At once I felt like a total moron. It was obvious how they knew. They had just done a mind probe on me, and had had a chance to check out everything that had ever happened to me—not to mention everything I had ever *done,* which, when I thought about it, was a pretty horrifying prospect. Suddenly I wished I hadn't let them do it.

"You see," continued the brains, speaking now

in unison, "during the training transfer Flinge Iblik's mind was actually physically linked with yours. When you severed the link before he had had a chance to withdraw, it left traces of his brain inside you—and probably a few bits of yours inside his."

"That's too bad," said Elspeth. "Rod didn't have any brain to spare."

I ignored her. I was busy rolling my eyes back, as if I thought I might actually be able to see the traces of brain that weren't mine.

What size traces were they, anyway? A few atoms? A synapse or two? Something the size of a walnut? A *baseball?*

"We're talking about subatomic particles," said the lavender brain, as if it had guessed my concerns. "They are carried on the electron flow of a training transfer. You could fit a billion billion of them in a drop of water. Still, they maintain a connection between you and Flinge Iblik that, though dangerous to establish, is very real."

Flinge Iblik was connected to my brain. Seymour had a direct line into it. The Ting Wongovia and the Mentat had both probed around inside it. I was beginning to feel like I should take reservations—or charge rent!

"As for the Ferkada, despite persistent rumors about it, we have never been able to confirm its existence, much less its location. If you actually discover any of this, please let us know at once. We regret we cannot help more in that matter. We will take custody of the monster, if you wish. As for BKR, he is a menace, and you should continue to try to stop him. You may leave now."

Grakker snorted in contempt, but didn't argue. He looked at Smorkus Flinders for a moment, then said, "May you be able to heal him."

At his signal, we followed the captain from the room.

I wanted to talk as soon as we left the Head Council's chamber. But our escorts were waiting for us, and it was clear Madame Pong and Grakker didn't want to speak in front of them. So we waited until they had returned us to our quarters. Once there we talked for hours. But all we did was go in circles. We had no way to untangle what BKR had said, to separate the lies from the truths.

Nor did we have a clue as to where to go next.

"Unless he was serious when he said to meet him at the end of time," I said. "But is there any such place?"

"A black hole might qualify," said Tar Gibbons.

"It might indeed!" said Madame Pong. "Come on, let's go back to the ship. I want to do some research."

With Grakker leading the way, we started back toward the *Ferkel.* But when we stepped out of the cellular elevator, we found Arly Bung waiting for us. Her face serious, she said, "We have just received an urgent request from the Galactic Patrol. They have asked us to hold you and your crew until further notice."

"On what charge?" asked Madame Pong smoothly—as if we didn't well know.

"Your ship has been declared a renegade, and your crew a danger to the general peace." Arly Bung paused. Then, looking nervous, she said, "Will you come without resistance?"

"Does the Head Council know about this?" asked Madame Pong.

"Security is *my* job," said Arly Bung, her gray face puckering as if she had just swallowed a cup of vinegar. "The Head Council does not have thoughts to waste on such minor matters. I repeat: Will you come without resistance?"

I held my breath, watching Grakker. Finally he growled but nodded his assent.

Given the fact that we were outnumbered by about ten thousand to one, that made sense.

Within seconds we were surrounded by Mental Initiates, who led us back into the cellular elevator.

This time we went down instead of up.

And down, and down, and down.

When the cellular elevator stopped, they led us into a round corridor that twisted and turned yet deeper into the planet. The walls were rough and fibrous, and I could smell damp soil.

"Where are we?" I asked.

"In the roots of the Mentat," said Arly Bung.

Deeper we went, and deeper still.

"Are we almost there yet?" whined Elspeth.

"We have to be almost at the bottom," I said, trying to sound encouraging.

"No matter how deep you go, there's always another level," said one of the guards. I couldn't tell if he was talking about our situation, or just stating the general motto of the Mentat.

Finally they herded us into a wooden cell, about a quarter the size of our room at the top of the tower. The walls were still wood, of course, but damp and soft.

The cell had no windows. Its dim light—about the level of late evening, just before dark—came from dozens of thick, glowing worms that hung on threads from the ceiling. Though the worms were well above the heads of the others, Elspeth and I had to duck to keep them from trailing in our hair.

It gave me the willies.

Arly Bung closed the door with a slam.

I heard the click of a lock snapping shut.

We were prisoners of the Mentat.

CHAPTER 17

The Hall of Statues

Now that our guards were gone, I steeled myself for an explosion of wrath from Grakker. After all, it was my reports of what I heard while in suspended animation that had led us to defy orders and come here.

We had risked everything based on what I said.

And what had we found?

Nothing, except disgrace and prison.

My stomach gnawed at itself. Had the idea to come here really come from Snout? Or had it merely been a hallucination after all?

If it *had* come from Snout, what—or who—were we supposed to find here? He had said someone would help us. What had we missed?

To my surprise, Grakker didn't say a word about all that, sent no hint of blame in my direction. Later, when I whispered a question about this to Madame Pong, she gave me that surprised look I got so often from the aliens.

"It was your suggestion to come here, Rod. But the decision was the *captain's.* He takes responsibility for his own choices. Otherwise, how could he *be* captain?"

I thought about that for a long time. Grakker was so cranky I always figured the crew was loyal mostly because they were the crew, and that's the way crews were supposed to be. But maybe there was more to it than that.

There was so much I had to learn.

A day passed, and then another. Now and then someone shoved food through our door. I wanted to stand up so badly I was ready to scream. But I didn't want it badly enough to get those worms in my hair.

To keep from getting stiff, Elspeth and I did exercises on the floor, stretching and bending as the Tar directed.

"I wish we had never come here," puffed Elspeth after one such session. "I don't like this place."

"Neither did Snout," said Grakker gruffly. "Which was one reason he volunteered to join the Galactic Patrol."

"The Mentat performs an important function," said Tar Gibbons. "But the place is out of balance. Warriors sometimes make the same mistake in the other direction, focusing only on the body and forgetting the brain. Warrior Science tells us you must balance the head and the heart, the body and the brain. Now if—"

The Tar paused. Closing its eyes, it appeared to be concentrating very hard. After a moment it whispered, "Someone is coming. Not the one who brings food. Someone else. She walks carefully, as if she does not want to be detected."

The Tar's ears were far better than mine, for it was several minutes before I could hear the footsteps approaching our door. Even then I certainly couldn't tell they belonged to a female.

The footsteps stopped outside our cell. A moment of fumbling and scratching, then the door swung open.

When I saw our visitor framed in the dim light of the root corridor, my heart leaped with joy. The flowing blue cape, the long purple face . . . could it possibly be Snout?

Something kept me from asking the question out loud, and as our visitor moved into the fuller light of our cell, I was glad I had kept my overly hopeful thoughts to myself.

But though it wasn't Snout, my first reaction had not been entirely foolish. The being who had come to visit us was of the same species as Snout—though female, just as Tar Gibbons had predicted. I knew she was female not from the way she looked, but because I had actually seen her once, very briefly, when my mind was linked with the Ting Wongovia's.

"Greetings," she said. "My name is Selima Khan. I'm sorry I was not able to come to you sooner, but getting past the guards was not easy. You are here because Snout called you, yes? Called *you,* in particular," she said, gesturing to me.

"Then it was real?" I asked, a flood of relief washing over me. "He really did call me?"

"Of course he did," said Selima Khan.

"Where is he?" asked Grakker. "Is he well?"

Selima Khan paused, then said, "He is with the Ferkada."

"You've been in contact with the Ferkada?" asked Madame Pong eagerly.

"I work for him."

Madame Pong looked startled. "The Ferkada is a single being? We had thought it was an organization. Who is he? Tell me more."

Selima Khan glanced behind her, into the root corridor.

"There is no telling when someone else might come to check on you. We should go now, while we can. We can discuss this while we travel, though it will have to wait until we are out of the roots of the Mentat. The walls here may not have ears, but even so, they are not entirely to be trusted."

"How do we know that you're not simply leading us into more trouble?" growled Grakker.

"You don't. If you would prefer to stay here in your cell, I will leave now."

Grakker's nostrils flared, but all he said was "Where are you taking us?"

"Back to the *Ferkel.* You have work to do."

He almost smiled. "Lead on!"

The first part of our escape was made in silence. With Selima Khan in the lead, we followed the root corridor around more twists and turns, then down again, then down again.

When we turned out of the last area that had any light our guide produced the alien version of a flashlight from somewhere in her robe. The tube was shaped like a thick candle. But instead of shining only at the top, the entire length of it cast a cool green glow.

Grakker pushed one of the rings on his shoulder, and the yellow midsection of his uniform began to glow, too.

"Holy utility belt, Batman," whispered Elspeth.

"Sacred mind, ruined by too much television," replied Madame Pong mournfully. I remembered that the aliens had told me they monitored our television broadcasts with a fair degree of alarm.

After that none of us spoke aloud, though Seymour felt free to talk in my head—most of it chatter not worth repeating. Edgar clung to my shoulder, chittering softly.

The walls grew narrower. I could hear water—or at least something liquid—running through them. They grew damper to the touch. Eventually the floor was so wet that it squelched beneath our feet.

I soon realized that not only were the walls getting closer together, but the ceiling was getting lower. Before long I had to stoop to continue walking.

And still the root got smaller, as if we were heading for its farthest tip. In some spots my shoulders scraped against the moist walls. I noticed that Grakker had to turn sideways on occasion.

The roof got even lower. Just when I was beginning to wonder if Elspeth and I would be able to continue, or if we were going to be stuck here forever, Selima Khan raised a hand to indicate she wanted us to stop. Setting down her light, she moved her hands over the rough woody walls.

An opening appeared.

One by one we stepped into the darkness that waited on the other side.

"Watch out!" called Grakker, who was the first to go. "It's a steep drop!"

"No matter how deep you go, there's always

another level," Selima Khan whispered as I went past.

When we had all dropped down, she closed the door.

Edgar, who had been fairly quiet so far, began to eeep nervously.

Can't you keep him quiet? I thought to Seymour.

I'm trying, I'm trying! hc rcplicd peevishly.

We were standing on a broad stone stairwell. The low stone roof that arched above us was carved with strange designs. To our right, the stairs led up, stretching as far as I could see in the light from Selima Khan's tube. To our left they led down, still deeper into Planet Mentat.

"It should be safe to talk now," said Selima Khan. "Though I think we should continue to move as we do."

Before anyone could respond, she started down the stairs.

"Were you the one I sensed watching us when we left the ship?" I asked, stepping down behind her.

She laughed. "You are very observant, Deputy Allbright. Indeed, that was me."

How come I didn't see her? thought Seymour indignantly. *Do you suppose she was invisible?*

Could be. I still don't know everything these Mental Masters can do.

* * *

I began to wonder if the stairs went on forever. Down, down, down we went. Eventually I heard running water again. Fifty or sixty steps later, the stairway came to an end at a dark, swiftly flowing stream.

"Is this good to drink?" asked Elspeth when we reached the edge of the water. "I'm really thirsty." She bent and reached toward the stream.

"Dip your hand in there and you may never see it again," said Selima Khan sharply.

Elspeth pulled back so fast she fell on her rump. "Why not?" she asked, her voice trembling.

Selima Khan shrugged. "Unpleasant . . . *things* sometimes swim through that water."

"How, then, shall we cross?" asked Madame Pong.

Selima Khan swung her light to the left. A narrow path bordered the stream. Just past the edge of the light the tunnel seemed to open into someplace wider and larger. I saw the shadow of a bridge, or at least a stone arch of some sort.

"That way," said our guide.

We had to walk single file, so we did not talk at that point. Whatever answers Selima Khan had for us, we all wanted to hear them together.

The water sounded pleasant as it rippled along beside us, until you thought about what might be in it. Once I felt Edgar's legs tense on my shoulder. I clamped my hand on him just in time to keep him from taking a dive into the deadly stream.

The arch was indeed a bridge. But I ignored it when we stepped into the area beyond the tunnel, because what we found there was so stunning.

I have no idea how large the cavern was, because I couldn't see the far side of it. What I could see will stay in my mind forever—partly because of why I could see it. For the instant we crossed the threshold of the tunnel, the lights went on. It was so startling that everyone except Selima Khan jumped in surprise.

I don't know where the lights came from. I don't know how they worked. I only know that the entire vast cavern, stretching farther than I could see, was flooded with a gentle, pleasant illumination.

It was lit, I am sure, because it was a masterpiece. A masterpiece of nature—its soaring stone walls were smooth and beautifully colored—but even more a masterpiece of art. Scattered across the vast floor, stretching to the ceiling, were the most colossal statues I had ever seen—bigger, even than the Statue of Liberty. They depicted all sorts of alien creatures, some in noble poses, some locked in titanic struggles. They were

carved so perfectly it was as if life itself had somehow been frozen in a moment.

"Who made this?" asked Madame Pong. From the awe in her voice I could tell that she, who had traveled the galaxy, was as impressed as I was.

"I do not know," said Selima Khan, stepping onto the bridge. "But I am glad they did, for it is a great wonder. Alas, we do not have time to linger. We must move on."

We walked across the bridge backward, our hands on the rail, staring back at the astonishing sculptures.

The bridge itself was sculpted as well, beautifully carved with leaves and flowers of all sorts. I trailed my hands along the railing, enjoying the feel of the carvings, until we got to the center of the bridge.

I stopped, frozen in astonishment.

At the center of the bridge was a post that rose higher than the others.

In the center of the post was a carving of a man's face.

Not just any man.

My father.

CHAPTER 18

Darker and Darker

MY SHOUT OF ASTONISHMENT ECHOED THROUGH THE vast cavern, the sound waves bouncing weirdly off the giant statues.

"How did this get here?" I cried. "What does it mean?"

In an instant Selima Khan was at my side. "It is a carving, like all the others. Why does it disturb you so?"

"Because it's my father!"

"That seems unlikely," she said softly. "This carving is several thousand years old."

"That's Uncle Art all right," said Elspeth, who had come up beside us. She hummed the theme music from *The Twilight Zone,* then said, "My father always said your side of the family was weird, Rod. Boy, he didn't know the half of it!"

"What does it *mean?*" I asked again. "How can it be here?"

"I do not know," said Madame Pong. "But I agree with Deputy Allbright. That is indeed a portrait of his father. I, too, find it very disturbing."

I barely heard her. I was running my fingers over the surface of the carving, tracing my father's features as I tried to make sense of all this.

The rest of the crew gathered around to look at the carving.

"This is a great mystery," said Grakker after a few minutes, his voice unusually gentle. "But we have no way to solve it now. And there is still a danger that someone may be pursuing us. I'm sorry, Rod, but we must move on."

The others started out, but still I dawdled behind, staring at the carving, continuing to run my fingers over the lines of my father's face, which I had not seen since the October night nearly three years earlier when he had vanished from our lives.

After a minute I realized I was crying.

"Where did you come from?" I whispered to the cold, carved stone. "What is this all about?"

Look, I don't want to make things too rough on you, interrupted Seymour. *But I don't want to get left here, either. I think we should move.*

Glancing up, I realized that the others had finished crossing the bridge.

I hurried to join them.

Selima Khan was talking to Grakker. "Let me assure you that you did the right thing in coming here, Captain. In fact, you just may be able to save the universe."

"From what? Smorkus Flinders told us that he and BKR were building a time bomb. But what kind of bomb could blow up the whole universe? And when is it set to go off?"

Continuing to walk, Selima Khan shook her head. "You misunderstand. They are not going to blow up the universe. When they say 'time bomb,' they mean *precisely* what those words imply. The point of the time bomb is to blow up time itself."

Elspeth laughed. "I've heard of killing time, but this is ridiculous."

"Laugh while you may, child," said Selima Khan sharply. "BKR, who has one of the most brilliant minds in the history of the galaxy, has worked out a way to disrupt the flow of time forever. If he sets off this bomb, it will divert time from its course. Instead of flowing forward, it will begin to move in a spiral."

As she spoke we entered a tunnel. The floor was covered with beautiful tiles. Shimmering murals lined the walls. Though I longed to stay and study the tiles and murals—both because they were beautiful, and because I hoped I might find another glimpse of my father—we hurried along. We stayed in a close knot as we walked so that we could all hear Selima Khan. As she spoke Edgar tightened himself against my neck. I had the feeling that he, too, was horrified by what she was saying.

"The time bomb's effect will start at the place where it goes off. But soon it will spread, spiraling first through our galaxy, then on beyond that, to the farthest edges of our universe. And as the river of time begins to wind in on itself, tightening down, the entire universe will begin repeating."

"What you mean?" asked Tar Gibbons.

"I mean we will begin living the same section of time over and over. And as the spiral tightens the section of time in which we are trapped will grow shorter and shorter, so that we repeat first a year, then a day, and finally a single instant over and over and over, eternally and without end."

She paused, then whispered, "Everything will be frozen. Nothing will change or grow again. The fiery stars will burn the same atoms over and over. The old person dying, the infant being born, each will be caught in that moment. The falling raindrop will never reach the ground. The opening bud will never come to bloom. Every being in the universe will be frozen in an endless now, some in pleasure, far more in pain, but whether in pleasure or in pain, all, all trapped forever and ever and ever by the death of time."

Her whisper echoed eerily along the tunnel. We stared at her in astonishment.

"Why would BKR want to do such a thing?" I asked, my voice dry as a corn husk in October.

Selima Khan closed her eyes. "He is infinitely cruel, and takes his joy in the suffering of others."

"He must have had lousy parents," said Elspeth.

"He is what he is," said Selima Khan. "As is true for most of us."

I don't get it, thought Seymour. *Won't this guy get caught in the time whirlpool just like everyone else?*

I asked the question out loud for him.

Selima Khan tweaked the end of her long face, a gesture so much like one that Snout used to make that the twang sent a pang into my heart.

"Indeed he will," she said. "But for him that is the irresistible beauty of this plan. The moment when he sets off his bomb—the instant of his greatest triumph—will be at the very center of the circle of time. This moment will be, without doubt, the most joyful of his life. And when the cycling stops—when time is frozen forever—that is where he will be: locked for all eternity in his moment of perfect ecstasy."

The horrified silence that followed Selima Khan's story made me feel as if the time bomb had gone off already. I thought of my mother at home, so worried and unhappy when I had had to leave. She would be doomed to an *eternity* of fearing for me and my father. I thought of the twins, never growing, never changing. Sometimes, when they were being cute, I had wished that they could stay that way forever. Now I knew I had never really meant that.

"How do you know all this?" asked Grakker at last.

"I have spent a great deal of . . . time on this matter," replied Selima Khan. "Most of my life, in fact. As Rod knows, I was enrolled at the Mentat at the same time as your shipmate Snout—"

"How do *you* know I know that?" I asked in surprise.

"I have been in contact with the Ting Wongovia. He told me the story of your adventures in Dimension X, and shared with me the results of the mind probe he did on you."

I decided that entirely too many people had had access to the inside of my head. However, I also decided this wasn't the time to complain about it.

"Unlike Snout and the Ting Wongovia, I did not complete my course of study at the Mentat.

As a matter of fact, I was expelled, for reasons I would rather not go into at this moment."

I looked at Grakker, wondering if he would be sympathetic since he had been expelled from the academy once. His face was expressionless.

"Shortly after I left the Mentat," continued Selima Khan, "I was given the chance to work on what was then called 'the BKR matter.' "

"What do you mean by that?" asked Grakker sharply. "Dealing with BKR was *our* job. Who authorized you to be involved?"

"The Galactic Patrol is not the only force working on the side of justice," said Selima Khan.

Grakker snorted derisively.

"A moment," said Madame Pong. Walking behind the captain, she did a module switch.

"The 'open mind' module," she whispered to me when she was done. "Not that it has ever been more than barely functional for the captain. But it may help some."

Sounding as if he had relaxed *just* a little, Grakker asked, "Is there any way to stop him?"

"Perhaps," said Selima Khan. "But it won't be easy. BKR needs two things before he can pull off this masterpiece of evil. The final item to finish his bomb, and the right place to set it off. He has chosen the location—a black hole located in just the right spot to amplify the effects of the bomb. But he still needs the final item."

"What is it?" asked Madame Pong.

She was silent for a moment. Then she took a deep breath and said, "He needs the brain of Rod Allbright."

"What does my brain have to do with this?" I cried, clutching my head.

"That makes no sense," said Madame Pong.

"You're not kidding," said Elspeth.

"Explain," ordered Grakker in his simplest, most captainly fashion.

But Selima Khan just shook her head and said, "I am sorry, Captain, but I am not under your command. Further information on this will have to come from the Ferkada."

Despite my pleadings, nothing I could say would change her mind on that point. Between the image of my father on the bridge and the bizarre statement from Selima Khan, I felt as if my brain was going to explode.

Well, if it does, at least BKR won't be able to use it to set off a bomb, pointed out Seymour, who until this point had been complaining because out of all the squintillions of possible sentient beings, he had managed to hook up with one who had a brain that was part of a plot to destroy the universe.

* * *

We were still trying to dig more information out of Selima Khan when the broad tunnel came to an abrupt end, sealed off by a pile of rubble, as if there had been an earthquake.

Without comment she led us to the right, to a small, rough tunnel that appeared to have been dug by hand. (Or maybe by claw. Whatever.)

The tunnel was so low that Elspeth and I had to stoop to enter it.

Grakker was asking Selima Khan how long it would take us to reach the ship.

I didn't hear her answer, because from the minute I entered the tunnel, my thoughts were distracted by a sending from Snout. It wasn't as clear and as simple as his previous messages. Just a sense that I should go to my left.

When I did, I found a small passage there.

I crawled into it.

What are you doing? shrieked Seymour.

Going to find Snout.

Are you out of your mind?

I don't think so, I replied, continuing to crawl along the passage, which was low and damp.

I could tell Seymour was following me. Edgar clung tightly to my shoulder, as if he feared falling off.

The message from Snout was so strong, so compelling, that I didn't think—then—about the fact that I was going so far from the others. It was as if I had gone into some sort of trance.

The tunnel branched, and branched, and branched again. Finally it spit me out into a space so pitch dark I had no idea where the walls were—or even if there *were* walls.

Only then did I realize I was totally lost in the bowels of a planet light-years from home.

CHAPTER 19

The Belly of the Beast

THE WAVE OF TERROR THAT GRIPPED ME WHEN I REALIZED what I had done was so deep and profound that I thought for a moment I was going to faint, or maybe even die.

Seymour took this as vindication of his caution.

I told you this was nuts, he sent into my brain.

"Shut up!" I snapped out loud.

My voice echoed back from the darkness, repeating eerily until it finally died away.

Well, at least there were walls. . . .

My intense terror had blocked the connection to Snout. Dropping to my knees, I took several deep breaths. *Stay calm,* I thought, remembering the first rule in Snout's book. *Stay calm.*

I repeated it over and over, until it became like a chant. "Stay calm, stay calm, stay calm."

Slowly my breathing grew more regular, and

my terrified heart stopped trying to claw its way out of my chest.

When I was calm enough, Snout made contact again. The connection was weak and confused. Following it was more like holding on to a guide rope than like reading a map—a guide rope that sometimes frayed so thin it almost disappeared. Without words the connection drew me forward. I stumbled through that dark and terrifying place, until at last I saw light ahead of me.

With a cry of joy I began to race toward it. But I had not gone more than fifteen feet when I stopped again, uneasy.

The rocks before me were arranged in a strange shape. I saw now that the light was a flame that danced in a hollow space almost like an eye socket.

Then the wall of rock shifted, and I realized it *was* an eye socket, the eye of a gigantic beast.

I turned to run, but the creature's tongue was faster than my feet. It wrapped around me. I am not ashamed to say that I screamed, over and over again, as the beast drew me toward its giant, gaping mouth.

The tongue was rough as a gravel road, but drier than I would have expected. It made a scraping sound as it dragged across the floor. I was squeezed so tightly that I couldn't move at all. Edgar was crushed so close to my shoulder he couldn't even *eeep.*

I expected the tongue to make a quick flip in and out of the beast's mouth, the way a toad's would. Instead it drew me in slowly, so that I had plenty of time to taste my own terror—and plenty of time to get a good look at the massive face surrounding the mouth into which I was about to disappear.

Seymour was running along behind me. *Oh, geez, Rod,* he thought. *Get out of there! Get out of there!*

I can't get out, you idiot!

Well, if you can't get out, then I'm coming in with you!

No! Save yourself!

I don't have any choice, Uncle Rod. Where you go, I go! I told you, I'm bound to you!

The beast's eye—the one eye I could see—opened and closed slowly, the great lid covering the flame, then revealing it again, making the light and shadows shift strangely around me.

The tongue drew me past a row of jagged, stony-looking teeth that loomed higher than telephone poles.

Wait for me! cried Seymour, scrambling between two of them.

*   *   *

The inside of the beast's mouth was like a cavern within a cavern.

The tongue drew me farther in, then suddenly flipped me back and into the throat, which was so wide that I flew through it without touching either side.

I landed in complete darkness, on something that felt like a gym mat. A convulsive motion rolled beneath me, pushing me forward.

The beast was swallowing.

The trip down the beast's gullet took longer than I would have guessed possible, and not just because every second felt like an eternity.

After a while I found myself chanting "No matter how deep you go, there's always another level." Whether I did this to keep from losing my mind, or because I had already lost it, I couldn't tell you.

The beast's gullet wasn't as wet and squelchy as I would have expected. But it was still too smooth for me to climb against the swallowing motion. (I know, because I sure tried.)

Well, this is another fine mess you've gotten us into, thought Seymour.

I'm glad you're here! I replied, relieved that I wasn't totally alone.

We're heading for a dissolve-your-flesh swim

in Lake Stomach Acid and you're glad I'm here? Thanks a lot! Friends like you I can do without.

It may seem strange to think of us talking like that, but you can only experience total terror for so long, and then something bursts. Now that I was sure I was going to die, I was just waiting for it to happen.

After a while we saw a light ahead of us.

What do you suppose that is? I asked Seymour.

Indigestion?

It took another several minutes before the inexorable undulations of the gullet brought us to the end of the tunnel. But instead of the terrible drop into a lake of acid I had been expecting, we came out onto—well, I guess you could call it a landing pad: a broad, soft area about five feet below the tunnel that cushioned our fall very nicely. We were in a space about three times the size of my bedroom. Its curving walls were slick and reddish. I decided not to touch them. The light came from a series of globes, each about two feet in diameter, that hung from the ceiling.

If I didn't know better, I'd swear those were electric lights, I thought to Seymour.

If you knew better, we wouldn't be in this mess, he replied, stretching his long neck so he could point his big eye in all directions.

Suddenly we heard a thumping sound. The

walls bulged inward a little, and we heard the rush of liquid. I jumped sideways, expecting to be crushed, but the walls soon returned to their previous position.

By the third time this happened I decided it must be caused by the beating of the creature's heart.

We got to our feet.

Shall we go on? I thought to Seymour.

Might as well, since we can't go back, he replied, blinking his big eye at me. *I figured we'd be dead by now anyway. Whatever time we get after this is gravy as far as I'm concerned.*

Staying close together for companionship, we traveled deeper into the belly of the beast.

The path—for there did seem to be something like a path that meandered through the center—led through chamber after chamber. Some of them were light, some were dark. In one we saw several bright yellow creatures that looked like lizards. They were bigger than I was, and normally I might have been frightened when I saw them, but I think I had used up all the fear that was in me—though if they had attacked, I probably would have found some spare fear around somewhere.

Instead of attacking, the lizards began to sing. Not in words; just sounds. Their music was weirdly beautiful, flowing and splashing. Whenever I try to hear it in my head now, I think of it as waterfall music.

In another chamber the path grew high and rocky, and stretched across a lake of bubbling, popping lava.

Ouch! thought Seymour as we started over the lava. *This is hot!*

It'll be a lot hotter if you slip and fall, I replied nervously. The stone path was no more than a foot wide—less, in some places. But it was all we had to follow.

We walked so long that every once in a while I had to remind myself I was *inside* a living creature. Once we even stopped to sleep. Hunger gnawed at my belly.

Finally we entered a large chamber lit not by the glowing globes, but by torches. Four torches, to be precise, jutting up from the four corners of a stone table about four feet high.

Lying on the table, silent and unmoving, was Snout.

His body had thinned somehow—not in the sense of losing weight, but as if he was in the process of disappearing. You could almost see right through him.

I rushed toward the table. Before I was halfway

there, a man stepped around the edge of it. He was dressed in a long robe and had a hood covering his head. His voice sharp, he said, "If you value his life, do not touch him! He must not—"

The man broke off.

At the sound of his voice, I stopped so fast that Seymour had to back up two steps in order to stand by my side again.

It couldn't be. Could it?

Sounding as astonished as I felt, the man cried, "Rod! What are *you* doing here?"

I said the only thing that made sense.

"I was looking for you, Dad."

Then neither of us said anything. We raced together and threw our arms around each other, and stood holding each other, there in the belly of the beast.

CHAPTER 20

The First Starfarers

IT WAS A LONG TIME BEFORE I COULD TALK. EVERY time I tried to ask one of the million questions pounding in my brain, it ran into a lump in my throat so thick that no words could get past it.

My father seemed to feel the same way. He kept saying, "I can't believe you're here. I can't believe you're here." But he didn't seem to be able to get anything else out, until he finally muttered, "Well, I guess we're a long way from home—eh, kid?"

I liked it when he called me "kid." It reminded me of the old days. Smiling, I replied, "We sure are, Pappy."

He paused, then said, "How is your mother?"

"She's not very happy. It was bad enough when you went away. It really broke her up when I went off to look for you."

He nodded, looking sad. "And the twins?"

"They're all right. I miss them."

"I do, too," he said, his voice heavy. "Now tell me: How in the world did you get here?"

"How did *you* get here?" I replied.

He smiled, put his hand behind his back, and said, "Paper, scissors, or stone?"

I lost, as usual. So I got to go first.

Dad listened with combined horror and astonishment as I told him everything that had happened since the *Ferkel* crashed into my tub of papier-mâché just a few months earlier.

"All right," I said, when I was done. "Now it's your turn. I want to know everything. Because there was sure as heck a lot of stuff you weren't telling us."

"Fair enough," said Dad. "But let me check on your friend here, first."

"What's the matter with him, anyway?" I asked anxiously, staring at Snout's fading body.

"We're having a struggle," said Dad. "He wants to leave this life, and I don't want to let him."

"Is that going to make sense after you tell me your story, or should I make you explain it now?"

Dad put his hand up for silence and pressed his forehead against Snout's. He stayed that way for several minutes, then stood and sighed. "Why don't I just tell you the whole story. Then you can ask whatever questions you still have. It looks like we've got time—though it's a long story, since it covers thirty-five thousand years."

"How can it go back that far?"

"Well, that's when I was born."

"What?!?"

Dad smiled. "This story is probably going to shock you, Rod. It may change the way you think about the world. I think the best way to get through it will be to let me just tell it."

I nodded and said, "I'll try."

He doesn't have to worry about me *interrupting,* Seymour pointed out smugly. *Since I can't talk.*

I mentally shushed him, and settled down to listen.

My father started again.

"I was born thirty-five thousand years ago, in a quiet corner of the galaxy, on a little planet called—" He paused, stretching out the silence until I was ready to burst. Finally he said, "On a little planet called Earth."

"Holy mackerel! You mean all that 'Chariots of the Gods' stuff you used to mock out is true? Aliens really did come to Earth a long time ago?"

Dad shook his head. "That's utter nonsense. To the best of my knowledge, Earth was the *first* planet to send travelers into space."

"Dad, thirty-five thousand years ago human beings were living in caves!"

"*Some* humans were living in caves," he replied gently. "Some of us had developed Earth's first great civilization. I don't mean me personally. It was a long evolutionary process, of course. Considering the fact that modern humans don't know we existed, except through misunderstood myths and legends, I guess it's possible there was an even earlier civilization that *our* people didn't know about."

The chibling eeeped. Somewhere above us the room-sized heart of the great beast continued its steady booming beat.

Of all the brains in all the dimensions in all the universe, how did I pick yours to connect to? thought Seymour

"So I'm not really half alien after all?" I asked, feeling both relieved and disappointed.

"It depends on how you define alien. In the eyes of the galaxy, I ceased to be an earthling a long time ago. Your bloodlines are half modern, half from ancient Atlantis."

"Atlantis?" I yelped. "As in . . . the lost continent?"

"Well, it wasn't lost in those days. And it wasn't really continent-sized. Smaller than Australia, but bigger than Greenland, to give you a quick idea. It was the center of civilization, and it was fabulous." He got a faraway look in his eyes. "I wish I could show it to you, Rod. We had conquered so many of the plagues that were ancient to humans even then: disease, hunger, war. It was a genuine golden age, and we intended to take it to the stars.

"Because I helped develop the technology to do that, helped figure out the key workings for our early rockets, I got to be part of the first wave of explorers. Now, you have to understand that as far as we had gone, we had not yet worked out faster-than-light travel. So getting around in the galaxy was still a matter of years—sometimes hundreds of years, at least by time as measured outside our ships."

"Time was different inside and outside the ship?"

He made a face and poked his index finger against my forehead. "Come on, Rod. Think! I taught you about relativity. I know I did."

"Dad, I was eight years old! Did you expect me to understand Einstein?"

"You *did* understand it. All right—quick review: The rate at which time passes is relative to the speed at which you travel. The faster *you* go, the slower *time* passes for you. Reach the speed of light, and it stops altogether."

I smiled. "Oh, yeah! I remember you telling me about that!"

"Good. Now, the galaxy—just our galaxy—is a

hundred thousand light-years from side to side. It has, oh, about a hundred thousand million stars."

Suddenly the words "Galactic Patrol" took on a whole new meaning. My mind began to boggle, as it did whenever I thought about these things.

"So we were doing most of our exploring locally—if you use that word in the galactic sense—traveling to stars within, say, a hundred light-years from Earth. But a round-trip like that would still take a few hundred years. If you wanted to go, you had to be willing to say goodbye to friends and family, because when you came back, they would all be gone.

"Between the time-effect that comes from traveling at near light speed, and being in suspended animation for most of the trip, we could travel for three hundred years but feel as if only a month or so had passed in the process.

"Of course, you knew a lot would change in that time. But it's one thing to expect changes. It's something else altogether to come home and find that your entire continent has disappeared and your people—not just your family, but your entire civilization—have gone to the stars."

His face was haunted, and I could tell that though this had happened 35,000 years ago in real time, for him the memory was still fresh and painful.

"They left no record, no reason for why they

left rather than just move to another continent. And there was no way to find them. It's not like it is now, Rod. With the crossdimensional shortcuts, you can get a message across the galaxy in a matter of hours, days at the most. But when our transmissions were limited to the speed of light it took eight years for a message to go round trip to the *closest* star. A message sent straight across the galaxy back then would still be traveling and not yet anywhere near the far side. My people—"

He stopped and put his arm around my shoulder. "*Our* people, Rod—the people who would have been your aunts and uncles and cousins on my side—could have been anywhere in the galaxy.

"My crew and I felt lost. Abandoned. And here's the strange part, Rod—or at least another strange part: Because I've spent most of my life traveling the galaxy at nearly the speed of light, locked in suspended animation, to me this story feels not like ancient history, but as if it all happened only fifty years ago."

I thought about that for a second. "How old were you when you started all this traveling?"

"About thirty."

"Well, even with all that other stuff, if it feels like fifty years have passed, wouldn't that mean you were eighty years old now?"

"I am."

"Wait wait wait! How can you be eighty years old? You're not my grandfather, for heaven's sake. You're my father."

He laughed, and I suddenly realized how much I had missed that sound, which used to fill our house. "Two things affect that, Rod. First, suspended animation itself seems to have ongoing effects which have slowed my aging. Second, in the greater galaxy, medical technology is such that—well, human life can be extended a great deal."

I nodded, thinking of the healing tables on the *Ferkel.* "Okay," I said uneasily. "Go on with the story."

"With Atlantis gone, Earth was inhabited by nothing but tribes of wandering savages. My crew and I decided to continue our explorations of the stars, hoping we might come across some clue to what had happened to our people. We became time striders, voyaging from star to star in trips that lasted dozens or hundreds of years, though for us only a month or so went by. We did the same thing over and over. In regular time thousands of years passed. For us it was only a decade or so.

"History rolled past us. Someone discovered the method for skipping between dimensions in order to leap across the galaxy, and after a thousand years of conflict the Galactic Empire began.

"Sometimes we would land on a planet and one of my crew would decide the place felt like home, or simply that he or she was tired of traveling, and so would choose to stay. Our numbers dwindled until finally I was the only one left. I could have stopped, too, I suppose. But I had no connections to hold me, and I had come to enjoy skipping across time like a stone across the surface of a pond. Going backward was impossible, or so I thought at the time. So I continued going forward.

"Now and then I would stop for a while. One of those times was here, on this planet, where I started the Mentat."

"*You* started the Mentat?"

He shrugged. "Bouncing around the galaxy the way I was, both in time and space, I realized that we needed a place like this—though I'm not entirely happy with how it has changed in the last few centuries.

"Of course, they've completely forgotten me now—don't even remember that my title as founder of the school was 'the Ferkada.'" He laughed. "But then, I started the place over twelve thousand years ago—six thousand years before the beginning of Earth's current written history. You can forget a lot in that amount of time. They probably don't even remember this beast is here, much less why we made it."

"You *made* this beast?"

Dad nodded. "It's genetically engineered, pretty much the same way as the giant plant that houses the Mentat." He narrowed his eyes and looked at me intensely. "Do you want to know why?"

Before he would tell me, he swore me to secrecy. Then he told me many other secrets as well, things about the world and how it works.

Things I am simply not allowed to talk about yet, though I hope to some day.

Which left three major items to talk about:

(1) How he ended up living back on Earth, marrying Mom, having me and the twins.

(2) Why had he left.

(3) What he was doing here with Snout.

Looking nervous and unhappy, Dad said, "Unfortunately, the answers to all three of those questions have to do with BKR."

I shuddered. Everywhere I turned, it was BKR.

"They certainly do," said a familiar voice. "In fact, maybe I should just pick up the story from here. Would that be all right with you, Art?"

I gasped and spun in the direction from which the words had come.

My stomach sank.

Oh, geez, thought Seymour. *Aren't we ever gonna get a break?*

Standing at the entrance to the chamber was BKR.

Looming beside him was Smorkus Flinders—not full size, but considerably larger than any of the rest of us.

Both of them had ray guns in their hands.

CHAPTER 21

Battle in the Beast

"A PAIR OF ALLBRIGHTS," SAID BKR HAPPILY. "WHAT a charming sight. Rod, if I had known what you had in your head back when I was hanging around in your sixth-grade class, I never would have smushed all those bugs against it. I wouldn't have wanted to knock it out."

"What *do* I have in my head?" I asked, trying to keep my voice from trembling.

"You mean your dad didn't tell you yet? Tsk, tsk. For shame, Ah-rit . . . keeping secrets from the boy that way. But that's the way you Mental Masters work, isn't it? Wrap yourselves in virtue, and keep everyone else in the dark."

"What are you talking about?" I hissed.

BKR smiled. "Your dad and I were working on a project together, Rod. Your dad's quite the genius, you know." He shook his head sadly. "Too bad he didn't pass it on."

Stay calm, I thought, and refused to respond to the insult.

"I *thought* we were working together, Rod," said my father. "That was before I learned the truth about what BKR is really like. He fooled me, as he had fooled so many others. As it turned out, he was planning something entirely different from what I had in mind. He just wanted to take advantage of my research."

"But what were you working on?" I asked.

BKR laughed. "Your father thought we were building a time machine. He wanted to get back to Atlantis, to see what had happened to his people. It wasn't a bad idea, actually. Start mucking around in time like that, and you would probably cause almost as much trouble as my time bomb will. But that's why I was working with him. Brilliant as I am—and I say that with all modesty—there were things your dad could come up with that I couldn't. We were just on the verge, right at the edge of what I needed to finish my bomb, when your dad up and disappeared on me!"

Dad snorted. "The very night I found the key to the problem, I also found out what BKR was planning to do with it. The research was far too valuable to destroy. So I fled with it."

"Just disappeared," growled BKR. "It took me nearly ten years to figure out where he had gone.

Who would have believed it? One of the greatest scientific geniuses of our time—of any time, given his history—hiding out on one of the most miserable little backwater planets in the galaxy. Married! With kids!"

BKR shook his head in astonishment.

"I decided I had been running long enough," said Dad, speaking to me, not BKR. "I met your mother, and I fell in love, and I finally gave it all up—the running, the searching, the bouncing through time. It wasn't easy—there were nights when I stood outside, staring at the sky, and longed to go back out there, back to the stars. But I had made my choice. I had a home, a wife, my children. I was settled at last.

"Then I got word that BKR was on his way to Earth."

"All I wanted was my missing piece of information," said BKR. "Just one eensy little piece of knowledge."

My father snorted. "One little piece of knowledge that would have let you bring time itself to a grinding halt."

"So you disappeared again," said BKR. "Leaving poor Rod and his mom and those adorable little twins all by themselves."

Lines of pain etched themselves in my father's face. "I disappeared to keep them safe from you, you abominable little monster. And it worked.

You had no idea they were connected to me until the *Ferkel* blundered into the situation, did you? You just admitted you didn't even realize who Rod really was when you were tormenting him."

BKR sighed. "I had clues that you had settled in that small town. But that you could bury your genius so completely; that the great galaxy-spanning time-strider Ah-rit Alber Ite could be living—happily!—in the boondocks, raising three kids . . . well, that did indeed stop me. A failure on my part, I guess. I'm weird, but this was even weirder than *I* could imagine. Besides, I was expecting *you* to be there. I have not had security leaks in the past, so I didn't even consider that you might have been tipped off I was coming. So with its missing father the Allbright family was not one of my prime suspects. Who was it that squealed on me, anyway, Ah-rit?"

My father smiled and ignored the question. "*My* mistake was that I *over*estimated you, BKR. I fled because I thought I could draw you away from my family. It never occurred to me it would take you so long to figure out the truth. I expected better of you."

BKR refused to rise to the insult. "Ah, well. In the end I figured out more than one truth. I know what you did with the information I want. Why don't you tell Pudge-boy here where it is?"

"What *did* you do with it, Dad?" I asked nervously.

My father closed his eyes. "It was important that I get it out of my head, Rod—in case BKR eventually did capture me. So I put it someplace I thought it would be safe."

My eyes widening, I put my hands to the side of my head. "You put it in my brain?" I shouted in horror. "You stored the information that would let BKR end the universe in *my* brain?"

Dad nodded, looking uncomfortable.

BKR spread his hands. "There it is, Rod. I need your brain to finish my time bomb, and there's really no way around it. I hope you don't mind."

Then he laughed—the same nasty laugh I had heard from him so many times when I thought he was merely Billy Becker, Boy Beast, the terror of the sixth grade. He made a gesture to Smorkus Flinders and the monster stepped forward.

He was about to put some of the same blue rings we had used to keep him prisoner earlier around both my and Dad's necks when the *Ferkel* came flying into the room. The ship was in its small size, which made sense for something that was going to be flying through those tunnels. Even so, I wished it was bigger.

Size didn't stop it. "Hold it right there, BKR!" roared Grakker's voice, blasting out through the ship's speaker. "I arrest you in the name of the Galactic Patrol!"

"Eat hot blast rays, Grakker!" shouted BKR.

He fired his ray gun at the ship. But the shields were up, and the rays splattered harmlessly off to the side.

The *Ferkel* fired back, but BKR, too, had on some kind of shield.

Squealing with horror, Seymour raced across the room and cowered against one wall.

Smorkus Flinders sprinted forward. Grabbing my dad, he jammed one of the blue rings over his head.

"Not him, you idiot!" shouted BKR. "Get the kid! He's the one I need!"

"Run, Rod!" shouted Dad. "Run!"

I didn't want to run. I wanted to wrestle my father away from BKR. But doing so wouldn't mean simply risking my own life.

It would mean risking the entire universe.

I ducked around the stone table where Snout still lay unconscious, and looked around desperately for somewhere to hide.

The *Ferkel* shot over the top of it and hit me with a blast of the shrinking ray. I began dwindling downward.

"Where is he?" roared BKR. "Where's Rod Allbright?"

Before the *Ferkel* could grab me with the tractor beam and pull me safely into the ship, Smorkus Flinders leaped over the stone table. He backhanded the ship, sending it flying against the wall of the chamber.

A horrible rumbling sound shook the floor. It took me a moment to realize it was the beast, roaring with pain.

Only two inches high now, I ducked into a crack in the stone table.

Peeking out, I could see that the *Ferkel* was in the air again, blasting rays at Smorkus Flinders and BKR. Swooping across the table, it hit Snout's body with the shrinking ray.

Nothing happened. It was as if his body was too faded, too nearly gone, to shrink.

Scrambling onto the table so that he could reach the blue ring around Dad's neck, BKR grabbed hold of it, then pointed his ray gun at Dad's head.

"Hold it right there! Another move from the *Ferkel,* and Ah-rit Alber Ite will no longer be the oldest living person in the galaxy."

I stared at the *Ferkel,* willing it to stop, praying for it to stop, so that BKR wouldn't hurt my dad.

The ship settled to the floor of the chamber. It was only then that I realized the floor was undulating.

I think we were giving the beast indigestion.

"Rod?" called BKR, looking around. "Oh, Roddie, where are you? Come on out, or I'm going to fry your father."

"Don't do it, Rod," called my dad. "Don't give him what he needs!"

"Shut up, Ah-rit," snarled BKR. "Let the boy make up his own mind. I think he's quite fond of you. I'm sure he wouldn't be willing to stand by and watch while I . . . well, no sense in being specific, is there? It will be more fun to surprise him. Shall we take a bet? I don't think little Rod can stand to watch more than two minutes of what I have in mind for you before he gives himself up."

I felt like I was being squeezed. If I didn't surrender, BKR was going to do unspeakable things to my father.

If I did, odds were good that BKR would be able to pry the secret information out of my head—information that I didn't know myself, even though it was stored in my brain!

My father's life, and the fate of the universe, were in my hands.

So I was relieved when Snout offered me another choice, horrible though it was.

CHAPTER 22

Seymour and I

I WAS STILL CROUCHING IN THE CREVICE IN THE TABLE when Snout whispered in my brain, *Rod, what are you willing to give up to save your father?*

Anything! I thought desperately. *Anything!*

If you're really serious, then I think I can help.

His thought-voice was so filled with sorrow that I almost burst into tears myself. Not that I was far from tears anyway. *What is it?* I asked. *Snout, what's wrong?*

The Ferkada has won, he whispered.

It doesn't look that way from here, I replied, glancing up at my father. He was still immobilized by the blue rings, held tight in BKR's grip. Then I remembered what Snout had said the other times he was in my head, that he was being held prisoner by the Ferkada.

Had my father really been keeping Snout a prisoner? That was hard to imagine.

I'll explain later, said Snout. *For now, here's my offer.*

I listened in horror as he explained what he had in mind.

Then I made my choice.

Creeping out from the table, I scurried across the floor to the *Ferkel.* Throwing myself at it, I clanged against the side of the ship. "Let me in!" I cried.

"There he is!" cried BKR. "Catch him!"

Smorkus Flinders dived for me. I was only two inches high now, and it felt like I was like being attacked by a mountain.

The door of the ship began to open. I leaped for it, caught the edge.

The ship lifted into the air while I was still trying to scramble in. I dangled from the door, and for a dizzying moment thought I was going to fall. But the training I had done with the Tar paid off. I made it in.

That was step one.

"Rod!" cried Elspeth. "When we lost you in the tunnel, I thought I'd never see you again!"

"This may be the last time," I said grimly.

Her face went pale. "What do you mean?"

"No time to talk now," I said. Turning to Grakker, I added, "Captain, please tell BKR we are willing to make a trade; one for one, me for my father."

"Rod, I don't think that's wise," said Selima Khan, starting forward.

"Trust me!" I snapped. "I don't have time to explain the whole thing. Just do it, before he fries my father. I guarantee, Captain, that this is going to bring *you* an unexpected bonus."

Looking at me suspiciously, Grakker turned to the speaker and said, "BKR, Deputy Allbright is willing to trade places with his father."

"Don't do it, son!" cried Dad. "I've had my time—more than enough time. Don't."

If I had had any doubt that he loved me, it vanished when I heard the agony in his voice.

"Oh, do do it, Rod," said BKR. "It will make me ever so happy."

It took time to arrange the terms of the trade. We had to get Smorkus Flinders and my father on one side of the chamber, and the *Ferkel* on the other. As the *Ferkel* set me down, Smorkus Flinders walked away from my father. The whole thing was set up so that neither side could pull back their trade at the last minute—as soon as I was out of the ship, the *Ferkel* was to fly over and get Dad. At the same time BKR would run over and put a set of blue rings on me.

We made the trade.

BKR put a blue ring around my neck.

Then Snout went into action.

Ready? he asked.

I swallowed. *Ready,* I replied.

Ready, Seymour? asked Snout, speaking in both our heads at once.

As ready as I'm ever going to be, he replied.

Then here we go.

It was just as Snout had said it would be. By acting as a conduit between me and Seymour, he was able to transfer the contents of my brain—every memory, every thought, every experience—out of my head and into the oversized but as yet underfilled brain in Seymour's stomach.

Just like downloading a computer, he promised.

I don't know how computers feel. As for me, I felt as if I was being sucked through a soda straw. Memories swirled around me—images of the twins, my mother, my father, our house, the swamp and the field and the forest where I loved to play. Pictures of school and friends, bursts of laughter merged with cries of anger. It was as if a thousand movies were playing all at once, playing faster and louder and brighter . . .

Finally I blacked out.

When I came to, Seymour and I were sharing the same brain.

This was not what I had in mind when I met you back in Dimension X, he said.

Oh, shut up! I thought fiercely. *We're not out of trouble yet.*

But it was nearly over. Chuckling at his triumph, unaware that we had snatched away the information he wanted, BKR told Smorkus Flinders to hoist my frozen body onto his shoulder.

At the door of the chamber BKR turned and said, "Remember, I don't need Rod's body—just his brain. Since it will be easier for me to get the information I need if they are both in the same place, for now I'll keep them together. But I can get at that information other ways, if I have to. If you try to follow us before we get out of the beast, his brain is *all* I'll take with me."

Then they turned and left, taking my empty-brained body with them.

The *Ferkel* settled to the floor. As the crew was climbing out, Snout sat up on the table and moaned.

Seymour and I trotted over to take a look at him. Or, to be more accurate, I went along for the ride, since I had no control over where Seymour went.

He's solid! I thought in astonishment. *He's stopped fading!*

That's right, replied Snout, speaking directly into the brain Seymour and I were sharing. *And*

I'm not terribly happy about it. I didn't want to come back to this plane of existence.

As soon as they were enlarged, the crew came running over to the table. They burst into a babble of questions. Lifting a finger to his long purple face, Snout said, "Shhhh. I'll tell you all about it when BKR is farther away."

Elspeth stared at my huge eye in astonishment. "Are you really in there, Rod?" she asked.

How do you put up with her? thought Seymour.

It's not easy, I replied with the mental version of a sigh.

We were back in the *Ferkel.* The entire crew had gathered around us as Snout explained that BKR's triumph was hollow. Though he had my body, my brain was empty. The information he needed to stop time in its tracks was still not his.

My father stared at Seymour—at me—in horror. "Rod, if you're really in there, blink three times."

Oh, please, groaned Seymour. *I feel like a trained seal.*

Just do it, will you? I thought angrily.

We blinked three times.

Dad let out a gasp.

"Boy, Aunt Jean isn't going to like this one much," said Elspeth, helpful as ever.

Snout went to stand in front of my father. The

sorrow on Dad's face was so intense that I wanted to cry myself—except Seymour was in charge of the tear ducts.

"I did not want to come back," said Snout.

My father nodded solemnly. "I know that, Flinge Iblik. But I did not want the Mentat to lose you. I felt the time was not right."

"It was not your choice to make," said Snout.

"Where were you?" asked Grakker, before my father could reply. I could hear a note of hurt in his voice.

"In the fields beyond," said Snout softly.

Selima Khan's eyes went wide, but then she nodded.

"What are you talking about?" asked Elspeth.

"I was dying," said Snout. "It started when we were in Dimension X, and I tried to find a friendly presence. While I was doing that mental search, I ran into something enormously hostile. I don't know what it was, only that the very act of touching it nearly killed me. Because I was in mental mode when it happened, I was pulled back to the Mentat. But rather than landing in the Mentat itself, I landed beneath it, in the belly of the beast."

"I suspect that is because I was here," said my father. "I was the one who first set up the 'recall' policy, back when I started the Mentat. The presence of my mental fields probably diverted the transfer to the belly of the beast, where I had come to hide from BKR."

"Be that as it may," said Snout. "The fact is that I had not much chance of returning to this life." He paused. "Do not misunderstand. This life is good. I like it here. I have good friends, beings I care about, care about deeply." He looked around the crew, acknowledging each of us, though I noticed that his gaze lingered especially on the captain, and on Selima Khan.

"But . . . once you have gone beyond, it is hard to come back." He sighed. "It is . . . interesting there. Frightening. And beautiful."

"No matter how deep you go, there's always another level," murmured Selima Khan.

"Precisely. But the Ferkada was not willing to let me go. I suppose it is just as well he did not, or I could not have worked the diversion that kept the vital information from BKR. But now I am weary, and though I am happy to see you all, I am quite confused, and need to rest a bit."

Moving stiffly, he left the bridge.

Grakker stared after him, the look on his face an impenetrable puzzle.

Tar Gibbons came over and put its hand on the snaky blue neck that I now shared with Seymour. "You did a brave and noble thing, my krevlik."

I nodded, and went to stand beside my father.

EPILOGUE:

Light-years to Go Before I Sleep

TWO NIGHTS LATER SEYMOUR AND I STOOD ON THE top of a cliff on Planet Mentat, staring at the stars with our single enormous eye. In the clear air I could see vastly more stars than I ever had at home.

Millions of them.

And somewhere among them—or perhaps temporarily in another dimension, taking a shortcut—was BKR. Was he heading toward the black hole where he had hoped to set off his time bomb?

Or had he discovered that we had fooled him, that my brain was useless to him, and his bomb wasn't going to work?

Whatever. The good news was, we had saved the universe. The bad news was, BKR was going to figure that out sooner or later.

When he did, what would he do with my poor, empty body?

Destroy it?

Use it for a dartboard?

Toss it into space like a piece of useless garbage, leaving me stranded forever inside Seymour?

Hey, you think this is easy for me? thought Seymour. *I had other plans for those brain cells you're currently using up, you know.*

And I had other plans for my life, I replied.

Below us, the crew was waiting. BKR was still at large, and it was our job to bring him to justice before he could cause more trouble.

My father came out of the darkness to stand beside us. Putting his hand on top of our head, he said again, "We'll find him, Rod."

Raising our small blue feet, Seymour and I shook them at the stars.

And I made my bitter vow.

This time it's war, Billy Becker! You've got my body, and I want it back. Wherever you go, whatever it takes, I'm going to find you. And when I do—beware the wrath of Rod Allbright!

Then my father and Seymour and I walked back down the hill, to where the *Ferkel* and its crew were waiting.

We had a job to do, and it was time to start.

About the Author and Illustrator

BRUCE COVILLE was born in Syracuse, New York. He grew up in a rural area, around the corner from his grandfather's dairy farm. Halloween was his favorite holiday, his school's official colors were orange and black, and as a teenager he made extra money by digging graves—all of which probably helps explain why he writes the kind of books he does. He has written nearly four dozen books for children, including *My Teacher Is an Alien; Goblins in the Castle; Aliens Ate My Homework,* and *I Left My Sneakers in Dimension X.*

KATHERINE COVILLE is a self-taught artist who is known for her ability to combine finely detailed drawings with a deliciously wacky sense of humor. She is also a toymaker, specializing in creatures hitherto unseen on this planet. She likes miniatures, and once made a dollhouse inside an acorn. Her other collaborations with Bruce Coville include *The Monster's Ring, The Foolish Giant, Sarah's Unicorn, Goblins in the Castle, Aliens Ate My Homework, The Dragonslayers,* and the *Space Brat* books.

The Covilles live in big, old house along with their youngest child, Adam, as well as a dog named Booger, and three cats named Spike, Thunder, and Ozma.